# THE SILVER COBWEB

NANCY DREW MYSTERY STORIES®

# THE SILVER COBWEB

## by
## Carolyn Keene

### Illustrated by
### Paul Frame

## WANDERER BOOKS
Published by Simon & Schuster, New York

Manufactured in the United States of America
10   9   8   7   6   5   4   3   2   1

NANCY DREW and NANCY DREW MYSTERY STORIES
are trademarks of Stratemeyer Syndicate,
registered in the United States Patent
and Trademark Office

**WANDERER** and colophon are trademarks of Simon & Schuster

Library of Congress Cataloging in Publication Data

Keene, Carolyn.
The Silver cobweb.

(Nancy Drew mystery stories ; 71)
Summary: Nancy's latest mystery involves golf pros,
opera stars, jewelry designers, and webs and spiders.

[1. Mystery and detective stories]   I. Frame,
Paul, 1913–     ill.   II. Title.   III. Series.
PZ7.K23Sil   1983   [Fic]   82-23723
ISBN 0-671-46464-7
ISBN 0-671-46463-9 (pbk.)

# CONTENTS

# 1

## New Girl in Town

"What a strange letter!" exclaimed Nancy Drew, half aloud. It had just arrived in the morning mail. Inside the envelope she had found a folded paper bearing an odd, scribbled design. This was accompanied by a note dated the day before and sent from an address in New York City.

> Dear Miss Drew:
>     I have often read news reports about the mysteries you've solved, so I'm hoping you can solve one for me.
>     Please see what you can make of this drawing. Does it suggest anything to you? The answer may be important!
>     I will phone tomorrow and explain the whole story.
>
>                     Yours sincerely,
>                     Tad Farr

The drawing consisted of a circular shape with curved lines shooting out from it on one side.

Nancy frowned thoughtfully as she studied the scrawl. "Those lines are so shaky," she told herself. "They must have been made by someone too old or ill to hold a pen steady."

Titian-blond with vivid blue eyes, Nancy was the daughter of distinguished attorney Carson Drew. Though only eighteen, her talent for solving mysteries had already made her well known far beyond the town of River Heights, where the Drews lived.

Her thoughts about the queer drawing were interrupted by the musical sound of the door chimes.

"I'll get that, Hannah!" Nancy called out to the Drews' housekeeper and hurried into the front hall. "It's probably Bess and George."

She had invited her two girlfriends over for Saturday brunch. "Hi!" Nancy greeted them warmly as she opened the front door. "You're just in time to give me your opinions about something."

"And do we have something to tell *you!*" Bess gushed excitedly.

"It'll keep." George Fayne grinned. "For a

9

minute, at least. What do you want our opinions about, Nancy? Don't tell me you have another mystery on your hands?"

"Well, sort of. A small one, anyway." With a chuckle, Nancy turned and led the way into the sunny, comfortably furnished living room. Bess and George followed eagerly.

Although the two were cousins, both Nancy's age, they could hardly have been more unalike. Bess Marvin was blond and dainty, but slightly plump due to her fondness for sweets. George Fayne was a tomboyish, adventurous type with a trim, athletic figure and short, curly dark hair.

"What would you say this represents?" Nancy asked them, holding out the strange drawing.

"Hmm . . . Could be the sun shining down . . . or maybe a spider," George ventured after looking at it.

"I'd say definitely a spider!" Bess declared.

Nancy nodded. "That makes three of us."

"Where'd you get it, Nancy?" George asked.

"In the morning mail. The person who sent it will tell me why later, when he phones." Nancy smiled at her friends. "Now tell me *your* news."

"Guess who's in River Heights?" Bess exclaimed.

"I give up. Who?"

10

"You'll never guess! Kim Vernon!"

"The golfer?"

"Who else!"

Nancy was genuinely surprised—and intrigued. Kim Vernon, widely regarded as the new queen of American women golfers, had burst onto the national headlines less than a week before, when she suddenly and mysteriously dropped out of the Charleston Cup Tournament without a word of explanation. Her withdrawal from the match was all the more startling since her total score at the time put her so far ahead of the field that she was regarded as a sure winner.

"How do you know she's in town, Bess?" asked Nancy. "Did you see her?"

"No, but George did."

"I went for a dip in the country club pool this morning," Bess's cousin explained, "and I saw her there with the club golf pro. I guess he's a friend of Kim's."

"That's right, he is." Nancy nodded reflectively. "I remember Buzz talking about her the other day, right after she dropped out of the match in Charleston."

"Does he know why she quit?"

"Far from it! He was as baffled as everyone else."

"It seemed such a shame!" put in Bess. "Kim was in the lead."

"I know," Nancy agreed. "And it also seems strange that he wouldn't give any reason, even when she was interviewed on television."

Still in her twenties, Kim Vernon had become one of the most popular sports figures in the country. Her rise to fame, since first attracting attention as a college golfer scarcely out of her teens, had been swift and sensational. A smiling yet intense competitor, Kim's good looks and cheery manner had made her a favorite of sportswriters and public alike. George Fayne was one of her most ardent fans.

"We might be able to see her play, if we don't take too long over brunch," George suggested eagerly. "Want to come, Nancy?"

"Sure, I'd love to! Hannah's making blueberry pancakes, and they must be almost ready by now. If you two will excuse me, I'll go help her set the table."

Bess was about to propose that she and George help too, when the telephone rang in the front hall. Nancy veered from her course into the kitchen to answer it. The caller, who sounded like a young man, announced himself as Tad Farr.

"Oh, yes!" Nancy said. "You're the person who sent me that strange drawing."

"Right. Can you spare a couple of minutes to talk?"

"Of course. In fact I'm dying of curiosity!"

"Good, I was hoping it might interest you."

Tad explained that his widowed mother had recently suffered a stroke, which left her partially paralyzed and unable to speak.

"What an awful thing to happen!" Nancy sympathized. "Is she the one who made the drawing?"

"Yes, and that's why I need help in figuring out what it means."

Farr related that his mother, an office scrubwoman who worked nights, had returned home early one morning feeling ill and had made an appointment to see a doctor the following afternoon. Since he himself also had a night-shift job, he had been able to look after her that day, except for about an hour when he left her alone to go shopping at the supermarket.

"When I got back, I found her slumped in her chair, hardly able to move," Tad went on, his voice breaking slightly. "She tried to talk, but all she could utter was a weak croak. Then she pointed at a pencil that was lying on a table near her chair. So I put it in her hand and got her a piece of paper, and she scrawled that drawing."

"In other words," said Nancy, puckering her

forehead, "you think she was trying to tell you something."

"I'm sure of it! In fact I think she originally intended to write one or more words, but when she found she had trouble even holding the pencil, she drew that as the next best thing."

Tad Farr added that he sensed his mother still wished to communicate an urgent message of some sort, and that her failure to do so bothered her a good deal. "If it's weighing on her mind, I'm afraid it may even interfere with her recovery."

"All I can tell you at this point," said Nancy, "is that the drawing resembles a spider—which probably doesn't help much. Or does that mean anything to you?"

"Not a thing. I'm really at my wits' end. Is there any chance you could come and see my mother in the hospital? You might be able to figure out some way to get through to her."

"Well . . ." Nancy hesitated, "if you think it would really help."

"I'm sure it would," Farr said hopefully. "Mom's heard about you and the mysteries you've solved, and when I told her I was going to get in touch with you, she brightened up right away."

14

"All right." The teenage sleuth felt she could hardly refuse such a request. "The hospital's there in New York, is it?"

"Yes, on the East Side of Manhattan," Tad replied, and gave her directions for getting there.

Nancy promised to see him and his mother during the hospital's visiting hours on Sunday afternoon, and hung up.

Over their brunch of blueberry pancakes and bacon, Nancy told her two chums about the unusual and pathetic situation that had led Tad Farr to send her the odd drawing.

Afterward, the three girls headed for the River Heights Country Club in Nancy's blue sports car, hoping they would not arrive too late to glimpse the famous woman golf star.

It turned out they were none too soon. As Nancy pulled into the country club parking lot, they saw a van bearing the name of a local television station.

'Uh-oh!" George blurted. "Looks like the news has already leaked out that Kim Vernon's in town!"

The three girls could see people streaming toward the golf course, which lay on the western side of the clubhouse. They hurried in the same direction. Apparently the TV news crew had in-

15

tercepted the golf star just as she and the club pro, Buzz Hammond, were finishing their eighteen holes of play.

Reaching the circle of onlookers, Nancy, Bess, and George saw a television reporter holding out his microphone toward Kim Vernon as she responded to his questioning, while the news cameraman, balancing his TV camera on his shoulder, recorded the scene on videotape. By now, other reporters had also reached the scene and were bombarding her with questions.

A friend told the girls that Kim, on seeing the television crew, had leaped off the golf cart she was riding and tried to flee into the clubhouse. When she realized it was impossible to escape she bravely accepted the situation and turned back to face the interviewers with her companion, Buzz Hammond, standing by for moral support.

Nancy noticed Kim's golf bag leaning against the wall of the pro shop, where the star had left it when she walked back to be interviewed. The white leather bag was easily recognizable with the pink initials *KV* blazoned distinctively on one side.

Suddenly Nancy's keen glance took in another aspect of the scene. A man was sneaking rapidly toward Kim's golf bag. The teenage sleuth's at-

16

tention was caught by his furtive manner and the way he kept looking over his shoulder to see if anyone was observing him.

She saw his hand reach out to open the flap of the pocket on one side of the bag.

"Stop it!" cried Nancy. "Leave that bag alone!" As she spoke, she dashed toward the sneak thief to keep him from stealing anything out of the bag.

With an angry snarl, the man turned to confront her. Nancy saw that he had a crooked, beaky nose and a drooping left eyelid, which gave him a squinting look.

The thief looked ready to strike the girl detective, but then he saw that other people were now turning their heads. So instead he unclenched his fist and gave Nancy a hard shove with the flat of his hand!

The blow caught her off balance and toppled Nancy to the ground, and her assailant took off on the run!

# 2

## An Unexpected Offer

Nancy landed with a thump on the thick green turf, shaken but unhurt. As she fell, she saw the squint-eyed man drop a small reddish object. But she caught only a glimpse of it, because the fellow snatched it up before running off.

Other spectators hurried to Nancy's assistance and several began chasing after the sneak thief. But he was too fleet to be caught.

One young caddy returned, gasping, "I lost him in the underbrush and shrubbery outside the gates!"

Nancy thanked the people who had come rushing to help her.

"Golly, are you sure you aren't hurt?" Bess inquired anxiously.

"Yes, honestly, I'm quite all right." Nancy laughed. "Thank you all again," she said to the two or three persons who were still hovering near.

"Well, I'm glad you're okay," George chimed in, "but your dress isn't. It has a big grass stain on it." She held out the white skirt to show the ugly green smear on it.

The interview with Kim Vernon seemed to be over, and she and the club pro were walking swiftly toward Nancy. They were followed by one persistent reporter who was saying naggingly, "Don't you think you owe your public an explanation for dropping out of the tournament?"

The golf star retorted firmly, "I'm sorry, but I've said all I'm going to say on the subject. Please don't pester me anymore."

Giving up, the reporter turned away with a grumbling remark under his breath.

As she reached the three girls, Kim said to Nancy, "I do want to thank you for stopping that fellow. I thought he was going to steal my golf bag." With a smile, she added, "I'm Kim Vernon."

The club pro, Buzz Hammond, put in, "Kim, this is Nancy Drew, our local super-sleuth. She and her father are members here at the club."

Nancy smiled and held out her hand to the pretty black-haired golf star. "I'm happy to know you, Miss Vernon. My two friends are dying to meet you, too. Bess Marvin and George Fayne."

After chatting for a few moments, Buzz had to leave to give a golf lesson. The girls turned to walk to the clubhouse, with George and Kim intently discussing the fine points of the course. The caddy picked up Kim's white bag and followed.

As they walked along, Bess remarked to Nancy, "That thief must have been crazy to try to steal Kim's bag in full view of all those people!"

"Well," Nancy said quietly, "remember that almost everyone's eyes were on Kim. We don't often get a celebrity like her at the club. Besides, I wonder if he really *was* trying to steal anything."

"He must have been! What else would he have been doing with her bag?"

"Perhaps he was trying to put something *in* it."

Bess gasped. "A bomb?"

"No, nothing that frightful," Nancy said with a brief smile. "But he did have something in his hand—something small and reddish. Whatever it was, it was important enough for him to stop and pick it up."

Nancy mused in thoughtful silence for a moment, wondering what the object could have been.

As they entered the clubhouse, Kim took her bag from the caddy, then turned to Nancy and her chums. "If you girls wouldn't mind waiting a few minutes while I wash and change my shoes, we could go upstairs and have some refreshments."

Kim was a soft-spoken young woman, whose sparkling brown eyes and relaxed manner the three friends found very appealing. She seemed genuinely to want their company. So Nancy and George smiled and nodded as Bess exclaimed, "Oh, that would be lovely. I'm parched! We'll go find a table."

Soon all four were sipping iced tea, while Kim kept them talking about River Heights. "I'm staying in a cottage near the river that a friend lent me," she explained. "Besides, I really like this town, and it's close to Bradley, where my brother lives."

The girls tactfully refrained from questioning her.

Suddenly George glanced at her wristwatch. "Oh dear, I'm going to have to leave! I promised my mother that I'd go with her to the eye doctor for her checkup this afternoon. Mom claims she can't see properly after she gets those drops in her eyes."

"I must be going too," Nancy said, "so I'll drop you at your house, George."

Bess decided to go with them, rather than miss out on a ride home.

"Can I drive you anywhere, Kim?" Nancy added.

The golf star declined, saying she had a car and also had something to attend to in the pro shop before leaving the club. "But we must do this again soon," she added with a charming smile.

As Nancy and her two friends were walking through the club lobby on their way to the parking lot, a stocky, middle-aged man called out, "Oh, Miss Drew!" and came hurrying toward her.

"We'll go on out and wait in the car, Nancy," Bess murmured.

After taking a moment to place him, Nancy recognized the man who had just called her by name. He was Simon Shand, a rather notorious businessman often in the newspapers, who had grown rich in trucking and shipping and who had recently, according to some unkind members, bought his way into the country club.

Shand was expensively and loudly dressed in a

22

wine-colored silk blazer and pink slacks, with a gaudy ascot knotted under his jowly jaw. Although he tried to be polite and amiable, his tough, ruthless manner tended to show through.

"Miss Drew, I saw you stop that thief a little while ago when he was after Kim Vernon's golf bag."

"Oh, did you?" Nancy said with a cool smile.

"Yes, and any young lady who shows that kind of spunk deserves to be congratulated. What's more, I hear you're quite a detective. So I'm offering you a reward right now—and a good-sized one, let me add—if you can find out who that hood was or turn up any information against him."

Nancy's curiosity was aroused. Why should this trucking tycoon, who was sometimes reputed to have connections of his own to the underworld, be interested in catching a small-time thief?

"Why, thank you, Mr. Shand," she said aloud. "I don't usually work for rewards. Crime detection just happens to be my hobby. I'll certainly do my best to try to bring that man to justice, though. But do you mind telling me why you're willing to pay for such information?"

"I'm just a concerned citizen, little girl, that's why." He smiled toothily at Nancy, but she

23

noticed that his smile did not reach his eyes.

The titian-haired young sleuth walked thoughtfully back to her car in the parking lot.

"Well, that didn't take long," said George.

"Come on, Nancy!" Bess giggled. "We're dying to know what that character wanted."

"Believe it or not, he offered me a reward to find the man who tried to tamper with Kim Vernon's golf bag," Nancy replied.

As she backed out of their parking spot, Nancy glanced in her rearview mirror. A slight frown creased her forehead as she noticed Simon Shand talking to Kim Vernon near the pro shop.

After dropping George and Bess off at their houses and promising to play golf with them soon, Nancy arrived home to find Hannah Gruen busy with chores. The kindly housekeeper had been with the Drew family ever since Mrs. Drew had passed away when her little daughter was only three. From that time on, Hannah had been like a second mother to Nancy.

"Ned's taking me out to dinner, but he won't tell me where," the pretty teenager shouted, leaping upstairs. "I have to get ready."

Hannah merely shook her head, letting a smile crease her face. She smiled again when the door chimes rang and Nancy flew out quickly to greet Ned and hop into his car.

"Still won't tell me where we're going?" Nancy teased as they started off in his car.

"Nope. But it's a restaurant that just opened, and it's not more than two miles from River Heights." Ned laughed. "Those are your clues."

It turned out to be called the Russian Bear, and Nancy was delighted with his choice. After they had made their selections from the delicious menu, Nancy found herself telling Ned about the sneak thief at the country club, as well as her encounters with Kim Vernon and Simon Shand.

When she finished speaking, Ned's eyes twinkled. "Well, I've got another surprise for you. Someone wants to meet you!"

"Oh, Ned! I can't stand any more suspense today. Who is it?" Nancy asked.

"Kim Vernon's coach!"

# 3

## Code Blinks

Ned's announcement took Nancy by surprise. "Are you serious?" she asked.

"Of course. Why wouldn't I be?"

"It seems such a coincidence!" I didn't even know you knew Kim's coach."

"I didn't, up till this afternoon. His name's Russ Chaffee, by the way. He was over at the Oakville Country Club, and the pro there introduced us."

Ned, an all-around athlete and star quarterback of the Emerson College football team, was to take part in a summer-vacation golf tournament organized by the River Heights and Oakville country clubs. He explained that, while playing the Oakville course to familiarize himself with its terrain and hazards, he had run into Chaffee and the Oakville pro on the eighteenth green. The three had chatted on their way to the clubhouse.

"As you might expect, Kim Vernon's name came up," Ned went on. "Chaffee said he was as mystified by her pullout from the Charleston Cup as everyone else. So naturally I boasted that my girlfriend Nancy Drew might be just the person to solve the mystery." Ned grinned and added, "Chaffee leaped at the idea—especially since he knew Kim would be staying in River Heights."

Nancy smiled, pleased at Ned's confidence in her sleuthing ability. "And just when and where am I to meet Mr. Chaffee?"

"Here. Tonight." Ned grinned apologetically at his date. "He had a dinner engagement in Oakville, but he wanted to see you as soon as possible. So I said tonight would be okay if he could make it here before eight-thirty. That'll still give us time to catch the late movie. I hope you don't mind too much, Nancy?"

"Of course not, if I can help."

They were just finishing dessert when Nancy saw a husky-looking man with thinning silver-blond hair walk into the restaurant. "Here he is now," Ned murmured.

As the man approached their table, Ned rose to greet him—"Hi, Russ!"—then turned to introduce the newcomer. "Nancy, this is Russ Chaffee, Kim Vernon's coach."

She smiled. "How do you do, Mr. Chaffee."

"Miss Drew, it's a pleasure." He sat down and, after the waiter had brought coffee, said, "I imagine Ned has told you why I've come."

"You want me to try to find out why Kim Vernon withdrew from the Charleston Cup Tournament?"

"Right. Will you?"

Nancy remained silent a moment, her pretty face becoming serious. "I'm not sure. For one thing, when Kim was interviewed today, she refused to give the reporters any hint as to why she dropped out of the tournament."

Russ Chaffee nodded and smiled regretfully. "Exactly—which is why I've come to you, Nancy."

"The point is, what chance have I of finding out anything if she's determined not to cooperate?"

Chaffee's smile gave way to a troubled expression. "Yes, I see what you mean. But surely, in all your mystery cases, you've had to cope with people who were trying to keep you from finding out the facts."

"That's true," Nancy conceded. "But most of

those investigations haven't been as personal as this, where the whole mystery concerns Kim's private motives."

Chaffee nodded again. "It's not an easy thing I'm asking, I realize that."

"There's also an ethical consideration," Nancy replied slowly. "I mean, if Kim doesn't want anyone to know why she dropped out, have we any right to pry?"

Russ Chaffee frowned and toyed with his coffee spoon. "I guess my answer would be that Kim's happiness is important to me, and I've a hunch she herself is pretty unhappy right now."

"You feel pretty sure of that?" Nancy probed.

"Put yourself in her place," said the star's coach. "You've practiced and struggled for years to become a golf champion. Now you've finally made it to the top, and this tournament is your chance to prove it. You're facing the best women golfers in the country and you're *beating* them— leading the field by a comfortable margin. The crown is within easy reach, so to speak. And then, just as victory is in sight, you're forced to drop out! . . . Wouldn't you be pretty unhappy in her place?"

Nancy was struck by his choice of words. "Why do you say she was *forced* to drop out?"

With a shrug and a frown, Chaffee replied, "I

just can't imagine any reason why Kim would quit of her own accord." Recalling the scene, he added, "I can tell you, she certainly acted mighty upset about it at the time!"

"Have you any theory of your own, Mr. Chaffee, that might explain what happened?"

He shook his head glumly. "Not a clue. The whole thing just doesn't make sense."

"How did you first become Kim Vernon's coach?" Nancy inquired.

Russ Chaffee explained that he and Kim's father had been close friends, so when she first showed an interest in golf, he had given Kim lessons that had helped her become a top scorer on her college team.

"After her parents died and she decided to turn pro," Chaffee went on, "I put everything aside to help her. I felt Kim really had the makings of a champion!"

Remembering the golf star's remark over tea at the country club, Nancy said, "I understand Kim has a brother who lives near here, in Bradley."

"That's right. Jack Vernon. Quite a promising young man. He's recently gone into politics."

"Has she any other interests outside of golf?"

"None," her coach declared. "That's another reason her withdrawal from the tournament is

30

such a mystery. If Kim had any aims or interests that conflicted with her golfing career, I might understand her dropping out of the match. But golf's her whole life!"

"What about romance or marriage?" Nancy asked.

"She had a steady boyfriend around the time she graduated from college," Chaffee related. "A young jewelry designer named Brett Hulme."

The name immediately rang a bell in Nancy's mind. "Oh, yes. He's quite well known."

"His workshop's near River Heights," put in Ned.

"That's right," Chaffee confirmed. "I expected them to become engaged. But then Kim became engrossed in her golfing career, which of course kept her on tour most of the time. So I guess they drifted apart and lost touch."

Despite her misgivings, Nancy promised to look into the mystery now swirling around Kim's interrupted golfing career. But she was determined not to do so in any furtive or underhanded way.

Later that evening, as she watched the movie with Ned, Nancy's thoughts kept straying back to Kim Vernon.

Kim had mentioned her brother's nearness in

31

Bradley was a reason for staying in River Heights. But now Nancy found herself wondering if Brett Hulme's presence near town might have been an even stronger attraction.

The next day, Nancy attended church service with her father. Afterward, over the appetizing roast that Hannah Gruen had cooked for their Sunday dinner, Carson Drew mentioned that he planned to drive to New York City that afternoon to see a client who was about to fly to Europe.

"Oh Dad, that's great!" cried Nancy. "I promised to visit someone in the hospital there this afternoon. May I go with you?"

"Sure thing. In fact I insist on it." Her father chuckled. "It'll be a treat having your company, rather than driving all that way alone!"

The gleaming high-rise hospital on Manhattan's East Side was crowded with Sunday visitors. Tad Farr, who proved to be a burly, freckled subway policeman in his mid-twenties, met Nancy in the hospital lobby.

"Miss Drew, I really appreciate your taking all this trouble to help my mother," he said.

The teenager grinned. "How could I refuse after you found such an unusual way to arouse my interest? By the way, make it Nancy, please."

"Thanks. You'll call me Tad, I hope."

As they took the elevator up to the intensive care ward on the tenth floor, where Mrs. Farr was a patient, Nancy asked if her ability to communicate had shown any improvement.

"Not yet, I'm afraid. She hasn't made any progress at all, as far as I can tell. But I'm sure she'll perk up a bit when she sees you."

Maggie Farr turned out to be a cheerful-looking woman with gray-streaked, carroty-red hair, whose lined face reflected a lifetime of hard work. As Tad had predicted, her expression brightened when he introduced the famous young detective. But Nancy could not repress a pang of pity at her helpless condition.

"Mrs. Farr," she said, "can you blink your eyes?"

The woman's lids fluttered up and down.

"Good! Now I'd like to ask you some questions. If the answer is yes, blink once. If it's no, blink twice. Okay?"

Maggie's lips seemed to shape a faint smile, and she blinked once.

Nancy squeezed her hand by way of encouragement and then took the folded drawing out of her bag. She showed it to the elderly woman and said, "Tad thinks you were trying to tell him something important with this drawing. Were you?"

Mrs. Farr blinked once. Emphatically, it seemed to Nancy.

"Does it represent . . . a spider?"

Again Maggie blinked once.

Nancy looked at Tad. "But a spider means nothing to you?"

He shook his head regretfully. "Nothing. I've no idea what she's getting at."

Nancy turned back to Mrs. Farr. "Is this a . . . a *live* spider you're talking about?"

The response was two blinks.

"Well then, a dead spider someplace in the room where you were sitting that day?"

Again, two blinks.

"A mounted specimen, perhaps, in a museum?"

Two blinks.

Nancy puckered her brow, trying hard to think of a question that might help the woman to communicate her meaning. "Maybe something that just . . . *looks like* a spider?"

Mrs. Farr's face brightened again and she blinked once.

Nancy's spirits rose, now that she had gotten another positive response from the patient. But

34

they quickly sank again when she racked her brain for a follow-up question and drew a blank. Nancy flashed a helpless glance at Maggie's son. "What on earth resembles a spider?" she murmured.

Tad shrugged and scratched his head. "Beats me. A little baby crab, maybe? Or some kind of small electronic part, with wires sticking out from it—except I can't imagine Mom wanting to talk about anything like that."

Nor could Nancy. "Never mind," she said, trying not to let her discouragement show. "Perhaps it would be easier if we could find some way to help her spell out words."

"Like for instance?"

"Well . . ." Nancy thought of Morse code, using long and short blinks for dots and dashes, but she had no chart of the alphabet at hand with which to instruct Maggie.

In the end, Nancy suggested they simply spell out the alphabet aloud and have the elderly woman blink when they came to the right letter, then start all over again to get the next letter.

It was a slow process. They had worked out three letters—*T-H-A*—when a ward nurse who had been keeping an anxious eye on the proceedings came over and insisted on taking Mrs. Farr's temperature. "I really think you'd better let her rest now," she said after a frowning glance at the thermometer.

Reluctantly Nancy left with Tad, after promising the patient to return another day. "I'm sorry I wasn't more help," she said when they reached the lobby.

"You did fine!" Tad Farr assured her gratefully. "I could see that Mom really appreciated what you were trying to do."

The titian-blond sleuth paused thoughtfully before saying good-bye. "Have you any idea what might have happened just before your mother suffered the stroke? I mean, while you were gone and she was alone?"

"Not really," Tad replied. "There was no sign of intruders or visitors. She was watching TV."

"What channel? Do you remember?"

Tad searched his memory for a moment. "As a matter of fact I do, because a soap opera she watches was just coming on." He named the show and the television station, as well as the date on which his mother had suffered her stroke.

Outside the hospital, Nancy hailed a cab and asked to be taken to the network skyscraper where the station had its broadcasting studio. Even though this was Sunday, she reasoned that at least a skeleton staff would be on duty to handle the day's programming.

Luckily the lobby guard recognized the famous young sleuth by name, and soon Nancy was talking to a woman staffer on one of the upper floors of the building. She asked what program had come before the soap opera on the day in question.

"Let me see. It should be right here in our broadcasting log." The woman flipped through a looseleaf binder. "Yes, here it is. *The Diet Chef* show."

Nancy sighed, swallowing her disappointment. "I don't suppose you'd know if anything unusual happened on the show that day?"

The woman shook her head. "I'm afraid not, dear . . . Oh, wait—there was something! According to the log, the show was interrupted for a special news broadcast."

"About what?"

"An interview with Kim Vernon. It was right after she announced her withdrawal from that golf tournament, even though she was way in the lead."

# 4

## Phone Threat

Nancy's eyes widened. For a moment she could only stare in silence at the television staffer.

"Are you all right, dear?" the woman asked anxiously.

"Er, yes. Sorry, I was just thinking of something else. Thank you for the information."

Nancy left the broadcasting studio almost in a state of shock. Could it possibly be that the urgent message Maggie Farr was trying to communicate had something to do with Kim Vernon or her withdrawal from the Charleston Cup match? If not, it was certainly an amazing coincidence!

But if not a coincidence, the alternative seemed just as weird. What possible connection could

38

there be between a golf star and a spider?

Nancy waited for her father to join her in a tearoom near Radio City Music Hall. Then, after a sandwich and iced tea, they drove back to River Heights.

Hannah Gruen greeted them with the news of a phone call for Nancy. "The same man phoned last night too, dear, while you were out with Ned," she added. "I forgot to tell you."

"It doesn't matter, since I wasn't in, anyway," the teenager responded with a smile. "Did he leave his name or say what he wanted?"

"Neither," Hannah replied with a worried little frown. "I must say, he sounded rather unpleasant."

"In that case," Nancy chuckled, "maybe it's just as well I missed him!"

She spent the evening curled upon the sofa with a good book, though much of the time her thoughts were far from the printed page.

"It doesn't make sense," Nancy said to herself for the umpteenth time the next morning, while dressing in a green knit shirt and a short green and white golf skirt. She was to pick up George and Bess and play a round of golf with them at the country club.

The teenage sleuth was still puzzling over the information that the woman at the TV station had given her yesterday afternoon. The intriguing problem gave her an additional reason to hope she might encounter the golf star on the course this morning.

Soon the three friends were well into their game, and Nancy was relaxed enough to be able to concentrate on keeping her two-stroke lead over George. As they were on their way toward the sixteenth green, Bess exclaimed, "Oh, look! There's Kim Vernon!"

Nancy glanced across the intervening row of shrubbery to see Kim waving a greeting to them from the adjacent fairway. She was playing with Buzz Hammond, the club pro, who was just selecting an iron from his bag.

In one way, it seemed a lucky encounter since it might provide an opportunity to follow up on her Saturday night conversation with Russ Chaffee. But on further thought, Nancy decided it might be best not to take any initiative in the matter, until she had decided how best to handle the situation.

Kim and Buzz had disappeared by the time Nancy and her two friends walked off the golf course.

"Oh, I'm sooo hungry!" said Bess. "Let's all have lunch here, shall we?"

George laughed and winked at Nancy. "When I'm with Bess, I never need a wristwatch. I always know when it's lunchtime or dinnertime!"

Her cousin giggled. "Oh, you're just jealous because I have such a good, healthy appetite!"

Nancy, who was standing by smiling at their exchange, found Bess's idea appealing. "How about you, George? Want to eat here at the club?"

"Lead on," the slender, dark-haired girl agreed willingly, and all three started toward the locker room.

Just then, Kim Vernon emerged from the club entrance. She declined the three girls' invitation to join them at lunch and said, "Nancy, may I speak with you for a minute?"

"Of course."

With a parting wave, her two friends went on into the clubhouse. "We'll go on and get a table, Nan," George murmured. "See you inside."

Kim and Nancy walked toward the shade of a big oak tree.

"Nancy," the golf star broke the silence, "Russ Chaffee told me he's asked you to investigate my dropping out of the Charleston Cup Tournament."

"Yes, he did. He's very concerned."

"Russ is a wonderful man and a good friend.

41

He's helped me a lot," Kim declared. "But this is my business only!"

The attractive young golfer's face was pale and serious. She spoke decisively, but Nancy thought she detected a faint tremor in her voice.

"I'm sure he only wants to help you," the teenager replied calmly.

"Perhaps so. But please," Kim persisted, "I must ask you not to interfere! I had my reasons for withdrawing, and there's no need to make a federal case out of it. It's strictly a private matter. So can't you just let things be?"

Her onyx-dark eyes looked intently into the teenager's sapphire-blue ones.

What a spot to be in! thought Nancy. Aloud and choosing her words carefully, she said, "I understand how you feel, Kim. I knew you might object, so I just told Mr. Chaffee I'd look into it—that's all. I assure you, you have nothing to worry about from me."

Kim let out a long breath. "Thank you, Nancy!"

"Sure you won't join us?" the girl detective went on. "We'd love to have you."

"I wish I could, but I promised to have lunch with my brother," Kim Vernon replied. "He's

42

driving over to River Heights on purpose. I'd better hurry, in fact!"

Nancy walked thoughtfully into the clubhouse and soon joined her friends in the dining room. Over soup and salad, she told them about Russ Chaffee's request and described her rather uncomfortable conversation with Kim.

"Does that mean you're not going to investigate after all?" George asked shrewdly.

The teenage sleuth shook her head. "On the contrary—now I feel I must. Kim didn't just sound worried, she looked frightened. I think she's in some kind of trouble!"

After dropping off Bess and George at their houses, Nancy drove home. As she entered the Drews' comfortable, cool hall, Hannah Gruen was on the phone.

Turning with a smile to Nancy, she said into the telephone, "One moment, please. Miss Drew just walked in. I'll let you speak to her."

Covering the mouthpiece with one hand, she whispered, "It's that man who called on Saturday and Sunday but wouldn't leave his name!"

Nancy nodded and took the phone, while Hannah retired to the kitchen. "This is Nancy Drew speaking. Who's calling?"

"Never mind who's calling," a tough, gravelly voice retorted. "You gave me a lot of trouble on Saturday at the country club, Miss Nosy Busybody! Next time you get in my way, I'll do more than just knock you down!"

And he hung up.

Nancy, too, put down the phone, her heart beating a bit faster.

Her unpleasant caller had to be the squint-eyed thief whom she'd stopped from tampering with Kim Vernon's golf bag! But how had he learned who she was?

After a cooling shower, Nancy put on a pink dress and went out to the garden, where Hannah was picking vegetables for the Drews' dinner. She told the housekeeper she had a visit to make but would be home for dinner.

"Good. We're having one of your favorite meals, dear—fried chicken and biscuits."

"Oh, great! I wouldn't miss it for the world!"

"You be careful now." Hannah smiled and waved.

Soon Nancy was driving out on Old Church Road. She had decided to talk to Kim's boyfriend, Brett Hulme. On the way, she reviewed what she knew about the talented young jewelry designer.

Over the past few years, Hulme had made quite a name for himself, designing special items of jewelry for prominent socialites and headline personalities. His work was sold in the most exclusive stores and had even been displayed in museums. Recently he had bought a big old house on the outskirts of River Heights and converted its ground floor into a workshop.

As Nancy turned into the graveled drive that led to the half-timbered, tudor-style mansion, she drove past a large, shiny dark limousine with a uniformed chauffeur waiting at the wheel.

Nancy parked and walked up to the house. Just as she reached it, the front door opened and a rather courtly, jolly-looking man emerged. He was elegantly dressed and had a beautifully twirled and waxed mustache.

Smiling at the pretty teenager, he doffed his pearl gray hat and gave a slight bow as he held the door open for her.

As Nancy beamed back at him, his expression made clear that he felt himself amply rewarded. Passing through the vestibule, she glanced out the wide front windows and saw him step into the waiting limousine.

Hulme's large, airy, sunlit workshop spread out over what Nancy guessed had once been most of the floor space occupied by the mansion's drawing room, dining room, and kitchen.

There were file cabinets, shelves, and work benches equipped with a variety of hand and power tools. Nancy's quick eyes took in buffing and grinding wheels, a drill press, a small lathe, electric pickle pots, and at various points on the floor a gas torch, a forge, a motor-driven tumbler for smoothing rough stones and metal, as well as a huge safe and a sink and counter all the way to the rear.

Hunched over a desk, with his back to Nancy, sat a broad-shouldered young man with thick, curly brown hair. Nancy caught her breath as she saw the beautiful creation spread out in front of him. He appeared to be assembling an intricate, weblike necklace. Its delicate, silvery strands glittered under the dazzling radiance of his work light.

With a start, the young man suddenly sensed her presence and looked up. "I didn't hear you!"

"Sorry." Nancy smiled. "I came in just as your last visitor was going out—that's probably why the sound didn't register."

The designer nodded and stood up, switching off the light and removing his eyeshade.

Nancy gestured to the silvery craftwork on his

desk. "How lovely! What exactly is it to be? A cobweb necklace?"

Hulme merely shrugged and folded his muscular arms. "It's a special order for a customer."

"Oh, I see. I'd better introduce myself, by the way. My name is Nancy Drew. I'm a friend of Kim Vernon's."

She saw Hulme's gray-green eyes brighten with interest, but his handsome face remained impassive. "Oh, yes?" Evidently the young designer was not going out of his way to make the interview any easier.

"I understand you and Kim used to be good friends," Nancy went on, "so I was wondering if you could help me."

"In what way?"

"Her coach is very much concerned about her, and frankly so am I. Kim has such a promising future, yet she seems about to throw it away. No doubt you've heard about her dropping out of the tournament in Charleston?"

"Yes, it was . . . too bad." Brett Hulme lowered his gaze uneasily and drummed his fingers on the desk. "Very unfortunate and puzzling."

"That's exactly the point," said Nancy. "No one can understand why she would do such a thing. That's why I came here, hoping you might be able to suggest a reason. You know her better than I."

Brett Hulme hesitated. His expression was troubled and sympathetic, yet strangely uncertain. Nancy sensed a conflict going on inside him, and for a moment she thought or hoped he might be about to provide her with a clue to the mystery.

Instead, he shook his head and murmured, "I'm sorry. I really don't know how I can help."

Almost as if in protest, there was a sudden crash of glass! A fist-sized object came hurtling through the window, straight toward Brett Hulme's head!

# 5

## An Ugly Brawl

"Look out!" Nancy cried and pushed Brett Hulme aside.

The missile flew past, barely grazing his cheek!

Without waiting to examine it, Nancy rushed outside to look around. When she came back into the workshop, she saw that Hulme had picked up the object.

"What is it?" Nancy asked.

"Just a rock. But it could have put quite a dent in my head! Did you see who threw it?"

"No. Whoever it was evidently ran off."

The handsome young jewelry designer looked somewhat pale and shaken, but otherwise unharmed except for a few slight cuts on his left forearm and cheek made by the flying glass. He allowed Nancy to draw him toward the sink to wash him off, but brushed aside her offer to bandage him. "Don't bother, thanks. They're nothing."

"Have you any idea who could have thrown that rock?" Nancy asked.

Brett Hulme shrugged. "Haven't the vaguest."

"You could have been seriously hurt! I think you should notify the police."

Hulme looked uncomfortable at this suggestion. "Surely it's not that important."

"How can you tell, if you don't know who threw it or why?" Nancy pointed out. "If you don't notify the police, I will."

"Oh, very well." Picking up the telephone, the young jewelry designer reported the attack and named Nancy Drew a witness. Afterward, Nancy continued chatting for a while, hoping to draw Hulme out on the subject of Kim Vernon. But when she realized that he would tell her nothing further, she decided to go.

As she was leaving, Brett thanked her for saving him from injury. "If your reflexes hadn't been so good, I might be in the hospital by now!"

Nancy smiled and handed him a slip of paper on which she had jotted down her phone number. "If you think of anything which might help to explain Kim's withdrawal from that tournament, I hope you'll call me."

Brett Hulme's face went blank again and he merely nodded in silence. Nancy drove away from his tudor workshop, strongly suspecting that the jewelry designer knew more than he was telling.

It was late in the afternoon when she arrived home. Nancy tried to call Tad Farr in New York but got no answer and concluded that the young police officer was probably visiting his mother at the hospital before going on night duty in the subway.

Nancy helped Hannah by setting the dinner table and making a big salad. Then she sat down in the living room to read while waiting for her father to arrive home from his law office.

Her glance fell on an article in the evening paper. It told about Jack Vernon and his campaign to be elected as a state assemblyman. The story mentioned that he and his supporters were holding a political rally that evening in the Bradley High School auditorium. Nancy decided to attend.

At dinner, she asked her father if he knew the young politician.

"No, I haven't met him yet," Carson Drew replied, "but he seems to have some good ideas. I'd call him a very promising candidate. Why do you ask?"

"I'm going to a political rally for him over in Bradley tonight. He's Kim Vernon's brother, you know."

Carson Drew nodded. "One can see the resemblance. He's engaged to marry Senator Hawthorn's daughter, I understand."

"Yes, their marriage is to take place just before the election," said Nancy. "But right now I'm hoping he can shed some light on why Kim dropped out of that Charleston Cup Tournament."

Promptly at eight o'clock, Nancy entered the high school auditorium. It was not full of people but held a very respectable turnout.

Suddenly, as she was about to take an aisle seat, Nancy gave a start. In the middle of the row just behind her own sat Simon Shand!

He did not notice Nancy, and she sat down, wondering what the trucking and shipping tycoon was doing at the rally. He hardly seemed the type to support Vernon's stand on various issues—especially environmental protection and the cleanup of toxic wastes. Still, the young sleuth reflected, people were full of surprises.

Jack Vernon soon came out on stage to a round of applause. He was a tall, dark-haired young man with an earnest manner and proved to be a good speaker.

"As you all know," he declared, "I'm in favor of laws to ensure toxic waste cleanup with some real teeth in them. I propose—"

"Aw, whadda you know about it?" a loud needling voice broke in. "We need some guy with experience!"

Thereafter, Jack Vernon was constantly heckled by five or six men scattered throughout the auditorium. It was impossible to hear him over their interruptions. Angry fights soon broke out between them and his supporters.

The political rally gradually turned into an ugly brawl. At last the police had to be called in. They quickly rounded up and arrested the troublemakers, but by that time most of the audience had already left or was streaming out of the auditorium.

Nancy waited until the lingering few who wanted to talk to the young candidate had done so. Then she approached him and introduced herself. "Mr. Vernon, I'm Nancy Drew."

"Oh, yes." Jack Vernon smiled and shook her

hand. "I've heard a lot about you, Nancy—all of it good!"

"I'm so sorry about the way your meeting was broken up tonight."

Vernon's face became a trifle grim. "Yes, it was deliberately engineered by someone. Not by my political opponent, I hope." His smile returned as he added, "But never mind all that. What can I do for you, Miss Drew?"

"As you may know, I'm a friend of Kim's. I want to help her if I can. The way she withdrew from that tournament when she was so far in the lead makes it hard to believe she wasn't forced to, somehow, against her will. So I'm wondering if you may know, or be able to suggest some reason that might explain why it happened."

Jack Vernon suddenly became very busy collecting his papers from the desk in front of him. "Sorry, I haven't a clue. Kim wouldn't tell me a thing—she just didn't want to talk about it. So that was that. If you'll excuse me now, Miss Drew . . ."

One of his aides had just come up on the stage after dealing with the police and reporters. Nancy realized she would learn nothing more at this time from Jack Vernon, so she wished him luck and promised to come to his next rally. "And please believe me," the teenage sleuth added, "I only want to help Kim!"

Because of the disturbance, the rally had ended early. When Nancy looked at her wristwatch under the streetlight, she noted that it was barely nine o'clock. She unlocked her car and drove home thoughtfully, pondering on who might have been behind the hecklers. She was inclined to agree with Jack Vernon that the troublemaking had been too well organized to be accidental.

The phone was ringing as Nancy walked in the door. She answered and heard Tad Farr's voice.

"Sorry to be calling so late," he apologized. "I'm on duty. This coffee break is the first chance I've had to ring you up."

"I'm glad you did," Nancy said. "I was trying to reach you earlier. How is your mother?"

"Not too well, I guess. The doctor will only allow me short visits. He thinks she's had too much excitement."

"Oh? What happened?"

The young officer explained that he had tried to continue Nancy's method of spelling out words by reciting the alphabet and having his mother blink when he came to the right letter. But the doctor intervened, feeling she was becoming tired and overexcited from the nervous strain and concentration required. "He gave her a sedative," Tad concluded, "and that's when he restricted my visiting time."

"Were you able to make anything of her message?" Nancy asked. "Or at least what she spelled out?"

"Not much. All I got was 'That girl' and then the letters *G-O-L-F-E*." Tad broke off as he heard Nancy's gasp of excitement. "Does that mean anything?" he inquired.

"You bet it does!" Nancy related her visit to the television station on Sunday afternoon after leaving the hospital, then went on, "If my guess is right, your mother was probably trying to say, 'That girl golfer, Kim Vernon'!"

Tad Farr sounded bewildered. "But why?" he asked. "What could Mom possibly want to tell us about *her*?"

"Has she ever met Kim Vernon?"

"Not that I know of."

Nancy was silent for a moment. She could not believe that her hunch was wrong about Maggie Farr's message being in some way related to the news flash that had been broadcast while she was watching television. The coincidence was just too

57

great! But what was the connection? Perhaps the answer lay somewhere in the past.

"Has your mother always been a scrubwoman, Tad?" she asked.

"Oh, no. Just for the last couple of years. Before that, she worked as a waitress. And at one time Mom was a dresser for that famous opera star, Madame Arachne Onides."

"*Arachne?!*" A burst of light seemed to flash in Nancy's brain.

"Yes, it's a Greek name, I guess," said the young subway policeman. "Why? Is that important?"

"Oh, Tad! It may be *very* important!" she cried.

"How come?"

"Haven't you ever heard that old myth?"

"What old myth?"

"In Greek legend, Arachne was the name of a woman who was turned into a *spider*!"

# 6

## A Famous Crime

"As a matter of fact," Nancy went on excitedly, "I believe the word for 'spider' in Modern Greek is still *'arachne'*! And that's also why scientists who specialize in the study of spiders are called *arachnologists*!"

Tad was as much amazed as the girl detective by the unexpected word clue. "You think the connection with Madame Onides' first name is more than just a coincidence?" he asked.

"It *must* be," Nancy declared. "There are altogether too many 'coincidences' cropping up in this case!"

But the explanation still eluded her. "Did your mother, by any chance, learn to speak Greek while she was working for Madame Onides?"

"Not really," Tad Farr replied after a moment's thought, "although now that you mention it, she did pick up a few words of the language. Some of them weren't polite," he added with a chuckle. "Madame O had quite a temper, I guess. But why do you ask?"

"I was just wondering," Nancy mused, "if that drawing your mother made after suffering her stroke might have been the simplest way she could think of to indicate the opera singer."

Tad was struck by this idea. But as she mulled it over, Nancy's instincts inclined her to doubt that she had hit on the true explanation.

"I'll just have to keep probing away at the mystery," she told him before hanging up. "At least this gives me another lead to work on."

Over a bedtime cup of cocoa, Hannah Gruen asked Nancy if Bess Marvin and other members of her amateur theatrical group called the Footlighters had won the honor they were hoping for.

"Oh, yes! Didn't I tell you?" Nancy replied. "They were chosen last Thursday to take part in the Oceanview Festival!"

This annual event was a week-long music and drama festival held in the pleasant seaside town of Oceanview. In addition to world-famous stars, various college and community groups were invited each year to perform in the outdoor amphitheater which had been especially built to stage the glamorous summer festival.

"That's quite an honor indeed," remarked Carson Drew from the depths of his arm chair. "I don't recall hearing anything about it on the local news."

"That's because the festival committee hasn't put out any publicity release yet, Dad. The official announcement will be made at the Footlighters' matinee tomorrow."

The Footlighters, under the direction of a veteran Broadway couple named Hamilton and Margo Spencer, made their home in a lovely old three-story house on the edge of town.

Next day after an early lunch, Nancy drove there with George Fayne. Both girls had joined the Footlighters briefly during one of Nancy's earlier cases, and they still helped out occasionally, though neither was as stagestruck as Bess.

"What's all this I read in the paper yesterday about someone trying to conk that jewelry designer, Brett Hulme, with a rock?" George asked. "The report said you were with him when it happened."

"Yes, it was rather scary—and definitely unpleasant." Nancy described the incident. Then she changed the subject by bringing up the Ocean-view Festival. "Have the Spencers decided yet what play they'll put on there?"

"Yes, that British mystery melodrama, A *Scream in the Dark*. You should be starring in it, Nancy!"

The girl detective chuckled. "Thanks, but I have my hands full right now with the mystery of Kim Vernon and that weird spider drawing."

"Speaking of stars," George went on, "did Bess tell you who's going to make the announcement today? . . . I mean about the Footlighters being chosen for the festival."

Nancy shook her head as she steered the car down the pleasant tree-shaded road. "No. Who?"

"If you don't know yet, I won't spoil the surprise," George said with a grin. "Wait and see!"

An artistic wooden sign hanging from a tree and bearing the name THE FOOTLIGHTERS marked their destination. Nancy turned up the drive and parked in the graveled lot which was already filling with cars. Then she and George joined the stream of patrons strolling toward the converted barn that served as the troupe's theater.

The Wednesday matinee featured a revived Broadway comedy that drew frequent laughs and hearty applause from the audience. After several curtain calls, the house lights went on. Then the tall, graying director, Hamilton Spencer, stepped forward with a smile.

"And now, ladies and gentlemen," he said in a deep, resonant voice, "may I present that world-famous tenor, Renzo Scaglia!"

A storm of handclapping, even punctuated with a few *bravos*, greeted the stocky, black-bearded man who now walked out from the wings. Nancy was as thrilled as George had expected. The darkly handsome Scaglia was not only a star of the Metropolitan Opera in New York, but also sang frequently at London's Covent Garden and La Scala in Milan.

He began by announcing that as one of the outstanding little theater groups in the area, the Footlighters had been specially chosen to take part in the Oceanview Festival. Then he asked Hamilton Spencer to tell the audience about the play which his troupe would perform there, and he urged everyone to sign up for festival tickets before leaving.

As a final touch, Scaglia brought down the house by singing one of the operatic arias for which he was most famous, "La Donna è Mobile."

When the exciting conclusion of the matinee was over and the audience had finally left, Mr.

Spencer introduced his guest personally to the Footlighters, including Nancy and George.

"Miss Drew is quite a famous young lady herself," he told the opera star. "Her specialty is solving mysteries!"

"Indeed?" As Nancy blushed, Renzo Scaglia fixed her with his deeply glowing brown eyes. "I believe I have read about her exploits."

"Very likely," said Hamilton Spencer. "She once solved a mystery on these very grounds that involved a weird dancing puppet."

He described the mystery, which was one of Nancy Drew's most unusual cases. Scaglia looked impressed.

"Perhaps the *signorina* would be interested in applying her detective skill to a famous crime that once occurred at an earlier Oceanview Festival," he murmured. With a playful smile quirking his bearded lips, he went on, "In fact I might even suggest to the festival committee that her sleuthing be used as a—how do you say?—a publicity gimmick to help promote this year's operatic performances!"

"Hmm, you may have something there," said Mr. Spencer. "What crime are you referring to?"

Acting on a sudden flash of intuition which she could never afterward explain, Nancy put in,

"Did it have anything to do with that famous diva, Madame Arachne Onides?"

She was scarcely prepared for the effect her question seemed to have on the opera star. His smile vanished abruptly. For a moment he stared at Nancy with a look as startled as if he had just seen a ghost. But Scaglia quickly regained his composure.

"Why not come down and view the scene of the crime for youself, *mia cara*?" he murmured suavely. "If you accept my challenge, I shall tell you the whole story!"

"I may take you up on that," said Nancy, returnng the bearded singer's smile.

She was still pondering Signor Scaglia's strange reaction the next morning when her boyfriend, Ned Nickerson, arrived at the Drews' home to pick her up in his car. Ned had asked her to play a round of golf to help him sharpen up for the River Heights–Oakville tournament.

"How's the Kim Vernon mystery coming?" he inquired on the way to the country club.

Nancy gave a helpless little shrug. "I'm not sure myself, Ned. But that reminds me—I have something important to ask her if we see her on the course today."

Privately the teenage detective realized that

her question might cause a few sparks, since Kim had requested that she discontinue her investigation.

As it turned out, Nancy heard her name called in the clubhouse soon after changing into golf shoes and before going outside again to tee off with Ned.

"Oh, Nancy!"

Turning, she saw the black-haired golf star hurrying toward her. Kim Vernon's attractive face bore an expression of muted anxiety.

"Oh hi, Kim." Nancy greeted her with a calm smile. "What's up?"

"I read about that attack on Brett Hulme. Is he all right?"

"Of course. He was just scratched a bit by the flying glass, that's all."

Kim hesitated. "I guess what I'm really asking, Nancy, is whether or not he's still in any danger." Her dark eyes searched Nancy's keenly.

The titian-blond sleuth was uncertain how to reply. "Do you have any private reason for thinking he may be?" she probed, turning the question back on Kim.

"Of course not!" A rosy flush crept up into the golf star's cheeks. "I mean, I . . . I just don't know. If some enemy is out to harm him, I only wondered if . . . well, if whoever it was might try again."

Seeing Kim's obvious concern and interest, Nancy could not help wondering if she now regretted having broken off her romance with Brett Hulme and was still in love with him.

They walked out through the clubhouse entrance, then paused as Kim said, "I might also ask why you were seeing Brett, Nancy. Did it concern me?"

The teenager's thoughts raced, trying to decide how best to respond. "I'll tell you that if you'll tell me something, Kim," she said at last.

"Tell you what?"

"Are you acquainted with Maggie Farr?"

"Maggie Farr?" Kim looked puzzled, then frowned slightly and shook her head. "Not that I know of. Why? Who is she?"

"A scrubwoman. But she was once employed by a famous opera singer." Something strange seemed to be taking place in Kim Vernon's expression. Noticing the change, Nancy pressed on. "She was a dresser for Madame Arachne Onides. Does *that* name mean anything to you? . . . or a *spider*?

Nancy was hoping Kim might betray whatever was going on in her mind by a few words or a look. But she was totally unprepared for the violence of the golf star's reaction.

Kim's facial expression dissolved into one of utter dismay. With a sobbing gasp, she barely stopped herself from bursting into tears! Putting one hand to her face, she rushed off toward the parking lot!

A moment later Nancy saw the golf star climb hastily into her car and go speeding off down the country club's exit drive!

# 7

## *Enigma in Red*

Ned was waiting to tee off when Nancy joined him. He had glimpsed the outcome of her conversation with the black-haired golf star.

"What's the matter with Kim Vernon?" he asked.

"Some questions I asked upset her," Nancy confessed ruefully, taking a deep breath. "Ned, I may be on to something that has a bearing on her withdrawal from the Charleston match. Do you know where I can get in touch with Russ Chaffee?"

"Sure, he'll be over at Oakville this morning, filling in for the club pro."

"Oh, good!" Nancy exclaimed. "Maybe I can catch him there when we finish our nine holes."

The pretty young sleuth called from the

69

clubhouse as soon as she came off the course. Although she was unable to reach Chaffee, the telephone operator at the Oakville Country Club promised to give him Nancy's message.

Then Ned drove her home, where Nancy transferred to her own blue sports car. Soon she was whizzing along the highway that led to Oakville.

Russ Chaffee was waiting to greet her as she pulled into the country club parking lot. "The phone girl said you wanted to see me, Nancy. Is it anything to do with Kim Vernon?"

"Yes, very much so. Where can we talk?"

"Let's go in the club lounge."

As soon as they were seated in comfortable wicker chairs by the window, with tall glasses of iced tea on the table between them, Nancy asked, "Does the name of Madame Arachne Onides mean anything to you?"

Kim's trainer frowned. "Well, I've heard of her, of course. She was that famous opera star. Died in a transatlantic plane crash, I believe."

"That's right. But you never met her?"

Chaffee shook his head, his expression somewhat puzzled by Nancy's line of questioning. "No."

"Was Kim acquainted with her?"

70

"Not that I know of. Why?"

Nancy described the strange urgency with which Maggie Farr had been trying to communicate something that seemed to concern Kim Vernon, but also to involve Madame Arachne and a spider—or something resembling a spider.

Russ Chaffee gave a low, startled whistle.

"Does what I've said ring any bells?"

"I'll say it does! Though I probably never would have remembered if you hadn't brought up the subject."

Nancy waited for the coach to explain. Chaffee told how, on a tournament trip to Florida, Kim came bursting out of her motel room one morning looking angry and near tears, and how he had seen her hurl away a crumpled-up piece of paper.

"Did you discover why?" Nancy asked.

"Yes, I picked up the paper and uncrumpled it, just to see what had upset her. Believe it or not, it bore a *drawing of a spider—in red ink*!"

This time Nancy was the one who looked startled. "How strange! Is Kim afraid of spiders?"

"Not that I ever heard of," the coach replied. "Which doesn't prove anything, of course. But that wasn't the only incident of its kind.

"During another tournament, in Chicago, she

71

didn't come down to breakfast one morning at the hotel where most of the players were staying. So I went up to her room to see what was wrong. Kim had been crying and wouldn't tell me why. Her eyes were all red and swollen. Then when she went in the bathroom to bathe her eyes, I saw this little transparent plastic box sitting on the writing table. *In it was a red spider!*"

Nancy was both intrigued and baffled. "Have you any idea how it came into her possession?"

Chaffee shrugged. "Only a guess. There was some wrapping paper lying nearby, with some postmarked stamps and Kim's hotel address on it. My hunch is, the spider had been sent to her through the mail by special delivery."

"I don't suppose that helped her game any," Nancy remarked sympathetically.

"It sure didn't! As a matter of fact, on both those occasions I just described, the emotional upset put her off her stroke completely."

"Can you remember any other such occasions?"

Russ Chaffee frowned and was silent for a moment. Then he rose from his chair to pace uneasily toward the window and back again.

"Yes," he said, "now that you mention it, I do

recall another time. This was in summer, almost exactly three years ago. Kim came on the course one day in the middle of a match, looking terribly upset, and . . . well, her game went all to pieces. She'd been tied for first place, but that day she bogied three times and dropped eight strokes behind! Black Thursday we called it. I remember it especially because most of the time Kim's a very cool, unflappable player."

"Any idea why it happened?"

"Not really. But now that you've got me digging up the past, something else comes back to me!" Chaffee remarked with a touch of uncertainty.

"What's that?" the young detective inquired keenly.

"You asked me if Kim knew that opera singer, Madame Arachne Onides. Well, she may have seen her at least once."

"When was this?" asked Nancy.

"On the evening of that same day I just told you about, when Kim got all upset and blew her game. The tournament was being held near Oceanview, and that evening Kim insisted on going to the festival, to see some opera that was being performed there. But, mind you, I'm not absolutely sure that Madame Arachne was in it."

Chaffee could offer no reason to explain Kim Vernon's sudden operatic interest.

Nancy drove back to River Heights in time to keep a lunch date with her father. Mr. Drew had reserved a table for two at their favorite Chinese restaurant, the Golden Pavilion. Over delicious servings of moo goo gai pan and tiny cups of scented tea, Nancy told him the latest startling developments in the mystery.

"Where do you suppose I could find out if Madame Arachne did perform on that occasion?" she mused aloud.

"Well, you might consult old Judge Drake," the lawyer suggested.

"Judge Drake?" echoed Nancy, looking somewhat intimidated. "But, Dad, you've told me he's one of the greatest jurists in the state!"

Carson Drew chuckled. "He's also one of our greatest opera buffs. You should see his collection of photographs and programs—and you probably *will*, if you get him talking on the subject! I'm sure he'd like nothing better than to have you ask him such a question, my dear."

"Well, in that case perhaps I will," Nancy decided with a smile.

Her father's prediction turned out to be correct. When Nancy telephoned from the restaurant, Judge Drake invited her to come over that very afternoon as soon as she pleased.

A valet ushered her into his large and old-fashioned but lavishly furnished apartment. Nancy noticed a bronze gavel on the mantelpiece along with framed photographs of his law school friends and legal colleagues. But most of the wall space was taken up with autographed pictures of famous opera stars and colorful posters announcing their appearances at opera houses throughout the world.

The retired judge himself, a short, heavyset man, looked like a jolly, gray-haired gnome with spectacles. He came bustling out of a back room with an armload of albums and opera programs.

"What a pleasure to meet you, my dear!" he beamed, putting down his burden to squeeze Nancy's hand. "I might have known that any daughter of Carson Drew's would have the good taste to be interested in grand opera! Now then, I understand you wish to know something about Madame Arachne Onides. Ah, what a voice she had! Without doubt, one of the greatest prima donnas of this century!"

As if to lend atmosphere to their chat, Judge Drake put a stack of her recordings on his stereo player. The room soon throbbed with her dramatic soprano arias. Meanwhile, the elderly judge showed Nancy numerous programs and other mementos of Madame Arachne's career.

"Do you know if she sang at the Oceanview Festival three years ago?" Nancy inquired.

"Three years ago? . . . Hmm." Judge Drake frowned thoughtfully and pushed up his spectacles, which were slipping down his nose.

He fingered through the material heaped on the coffee table in front of them. At last he came up with a festival-week program as large and thick as a good-sized magazine. "Ah, here we are. Yes, Arachne Onides sang in all three operas that were performed that year. Which one were you interested in?"

The one that was staged on a Thursday evening."

"Thursday? But that's not possible. The festival operas are always staged on the same days every year—one on the Saturday that opens the festival, one on Wednesday of the ensuing week, and one on the closing Saturday night."

Nancy was startled. From the way Russ Chaffee had spoken of "Black Thursday," it seemed unlikely that he had misremembered the day.

"What about the Wednesday performance, then?" Nancy queried after a pause.

76

"That would have been . . . let me see." Judge Drake leafed through the pages of the program. "Ah yes, *Carmen*."

Nancy looked at the names in the cast. Madame Arachne, of course, had starred as Carmen. And the tenor who sang the role of Don José had been Renzo Scaglia!

It was almost an hour later when Nancy was finally able to break away, after thanking her elderly host. She had an idea which might be farfetched yet seemed worth investigating.

From the judge's condominium, she drove to a large wooded estate near River Heights. The sprawling stone house, with glassed-in greenhouse extensions on two sides, was the home of a noted arachnologist named Paul Taggart. Schoolchildren often came here with their teachers to see his fascinating collection of live and mounted specimens. Nancy herself remembered such a visit by her ninth-grade science class.

Taggart, in turn, had read several news stories about the pretty young sleuth's exciting mystery cases. When Nancy explained why she had come, he was more than willing to help.

"A red spider?" Taggart mused. "Well now, red or reddish brown is certainly not an unusual color for spiders. In fact certain varieties, such as this Australian Nicodamus, or this Jamaican orb weaver hanging from its web over there, may be a quite brilliant red."

"Then the color itself doesn't suggest anything in particular to you?" asked Nancy.

The tall, slender expert shook his head, with its bushy mop of sandy, graying hair. "None that I can think of. There are many superstitions about spiders, for instance, but I can't think of any that concern their color alone."

Taggart stopped short and flashed a sudden puzzled glance at Nancy.

"Didn't I read something in the paper recently about a mysterious attack on that young jewelry designer, Brett Hulme, while you were in his shop?"

Nancy nodded. "Yes, why?"

"Well, there may be no connection, but I recall Hulme coming here some time ago, to look at various kinds of red spiders!"

# 8

## Trail to Nowhere

Nancy's eyes widened on hearing this startling information. "Did Brett Hulme give any reason for his interest?"

"No . . . but as I recall he brought along a sketchpad and made drawings of several specimens." Taggart reflected a moment and added, "I think he came hoping to see some particular kind of spider, and he seemed disappointed that he couldn't find exactly what he was looking for."

"How long ago did this happen?"

"Oh, I'd say three or four years ago."

Nancy drove home thoughtfully. The spider expert had just provided a second link connecting Brett Hulme to the mystery, and her sleuthing instinct told her it might well prove important. But the time frame puzzled her. Nancy could not forget the beautiful silvery cobweb she had glimpsed only recently on Brett's workbench.

The rest of Nancy's afternoon was taken up with running errands for Hannah and answering a pile of letters, a job she had not had time to attend to for a while.

For a change, she spent a quiet evening at home, reading and watching television. By giving her mind a rest from the mystery, Nancy hoped, she could return to the case refreshed.

The next morning, Nancy picked up George Fayne and Bess Marvin, and the three girls drove to the Footlighters' barn theater.

"I wonder what job they'll give me to do?" George wondered aloud. She and Nancy had volunteered to help the group prepare for its performance at the Oceanview Festival.

"Search me," Bess replied. "But I do know they want Nancy to watch the play and learn Connie Phelps' lines."

George shuddered. "Count me out of anything onstage! I have this absolute faith I'd make an idiot of myself in front of an audience!"

As the girls pulled into the Footlighters' parking lot, voices could be heard from the barn theater as members busied themselves checking out and refurbishing props and costumes for the mystery melodrama, *A Scream in the Dark*, which was to be staged at the festival.

Later, Hamilton and Margo Spencer rehearsed the cast on some scenes that needed polishing. Nancy sat and listened and watched.

"It's awfully difficult to learn a play this way, Nancy," Mrs. Spencer said, slipping into the seat next to the young sleuth.

"Yes, but I'm getting a good idea of what to do and what not to do." Nancy laughed.

"Suppose I give you a script to take home and study."

"That would be great."

"It always helps to know we have a good understudy ready to step into a part," Margo went on. "Judging by your past performances, we'll have no worry about this one."

"She's right, Nancy." Hamilton Spencer had joined them. "I wish you'd consider acting in our productions regularly. You have too much talent not to put it to use."

Nancy blushed. "Unfortunately, solving mysteries doesn't leave me much spare time."

"Do think about it, though, dear," Mrs. Spencer said, patting her arm.

During a break in the rehearsal, Nancy filled in Bess and George on the progress of her investigation. "I can't help wondering," she mused, "if this spider thing may have had something to do with breaking up the romance between Brett Hulme and Kim."

"I doubt it," George said firmly. "If you ask me, it was more a problem of career versus marriage."

"What makes you so sure?"

"Listen, if that's what George thinks, it must be so!" Bess put in with a laugh. "She's been following Kim Vernon's career ever since she broke into golf. I think she's Kim's biggest fan!"

"Come to think of it," said George, "I remember an interview in a sports magazine where she talked about that very subject. I may still have it."

"I'd like to read it, if you do," Nancy said.

"Okay, I'll look it up at lunchtime. Why don't you two come home and eat with me?"

"What's on the menu?" Bess inquired, then turned to Nancy with a giggle. "You know how George is—she's always trying to get me to eat carrot sticks and lettuce!"

"Don't worry, cousin dear. We'll have cold

chicken and ham and cheese and German potato salad and homemade bread."

"Oh, yummy!" Bess squealed.

The girls ate their lunch on the sunny patio in back of George's house. Afterward, George went inside to try to find the sports magazine she had referred to. Minutes later she emerged, waving it in her hand.

"Ta-da! Here, see for yourself what Kim says, Nancy."

The teenage detective scanned the article with interest. It confirmed what George had said at the barn theater. Reading the interview, Nancy felt that Kim Vernon sounded bitter. She had said that a professional golfing career would never mix with marriage, because the average husband would never put up with a wife who had to spend so much time on tour, away from home.

"Well, what'd I tell you?" George inquired as Nancy looked up from the magazine.

"Very interesting."

Later that afternoon, when the Footlighters broke off for the day, Nancy decided to pay another visit to Brett Hulme's workshop before going home. As she entered, the young designer looked up with a friendly, if guarded, smile.

This time, Nancy caught no shimmer of silver on his desk: it was a heavy gold-link bracelet that he was working on.

"More sleuthing?"

"A little." Nancy smile apologetically. "But that's not the only reason I came."

Switching off his worklight, Brett led her to an alcove with some comfortable chairs where they could sit and talk.

"Kim was very upset when she read about the close call you had with that rock thrown through your window," Nancy began.

From the way Brett Hulme's eyes had kindled with interest as she spoke, Nancy felt more certain than ever that he still cared for Kim Vernon. But he remained awkwardly silent. However, as she introduced the subject of the magazine interview, Brett gradually relaxed and began to talk.

"Yes, Kim and I were engaged. And it's all my fault that we broke up," he confessed unhappily. "I made the mistake of pressuring her. You know, insisting that she give up golf or cut down on tournaments, that sort of thing. I was selfish. I didn't realize how hard Kim had worked to get where she was. Of course I know better now."

Hoping that she had gained Brett's confidence, Nancy at last mentioned her chat with Paul Taggart. "He said that you once came to look over his red spider specimens. Would you mind telling me why?"

At her unexpected question, Brett Hulme seemed to freeze up. A trapped, suspicious look flickered across his face.

At that moment, the telephone rang, saving Brett from replying. Nancy thought that he looked relieved at the interruption. He sprang toward the phone, and lifted the receiver.

Evidently Brett found the call rather unpleasant as well, judging by his disturbed expression. His guarded remarks were made in a low voice. Nancy was only able to hear him address his caller as Mr. Shand and later say, "All right." Then he hung up.

Turning to Nancy, he said curtly, "I'm sorry if I seem rude, but something important has come up, and I have to go see someone right away."

"Of course. I understand," Nancy said politely. She rose from her chair and, saying good-bye, went out to her car. But the call had aroused her curiosity, and she decided to see where Brett Hulme had to go in such a hurry.

Turning out of his drive, Nancy went only a little way down the road, then pulled over among some trees at a point where she could watch his house. Screened by the roadside shrubbery, she waited for Hulme to emerge.

Presently a white car exited from his drive. But instead of turning in Nancy's direction, back toward River Heights, it headed the other way.

Where is he going? Nancy wondered.

Keying her engine back to life, she started to follow him cautiously. The road dead-ended only a mile or so away on a pleasant promontory overlooking the river.

Nancy turned off quickly onto a little-used dirt path that was heavily overgrown with vines and brush. Then she stopped her car again, got out and made her way on foot to a spot where she could see what was going on without being seen herself.

Brett had parked his car and was pacing back and forth on the promontory, hands thrust deep into his pockets, and a brooding expression on his face. Was he thinking of Kim?

Nancy watched patiently from behind her screen of trees and shrubbery, thinking he might be waiting to meet someone. But after ten minutes or so, Brett merely stepped into his car, maneuvered it in reverse and headed back the way he had come.

Nancy hastily returned to her own car and re-

sumed trailing him, although he was now out of
sight. As his workshop came into view, she was
just in time to see his white car pulling around to
the back of the house.

So his story about meeting someone had been
just an excuse to avoid answering her question
about his interest in red spiders!

Still puzzled, but encouraged that she was at
least on the right track, Nancy drove home.

But a frightening sight awaited the teenage
sleuth as she unlocked the door of the Drews'
house and entered the front hall.

Hannah Gruen was lying motionless on the
floor!

# 9

## Scaglia Changes His Tune

Even as Nancy felt Hannah's pulse and found it strong and steady, the housekeeper groaned and moved her head.

Nancy rushed into the kitchen and held a tea towel under the cold water tap, then wrung it out and rushed back to to put it on Hannah's forehead. The woman's eyes fluttered open.

"Oh, Hannah, are you all right? No, don't move just yet." she said. "Tell me what happened."

"Nancy, I just went out in the garden to pick some tomatoes. And then, soon after I came back in the house, I heard a noise in the living room."

"Who was it?" Nancy asked, helping the housekeeper to sit up. "An intruder?"

"Yes! As I came through the hall, a man rushed out of the living room. He bumped into me so hard he knocked me over! I guess I must have hit my head when I fell." Hannah gingerly felt the sore spot with her hand.

"Do you feel well enough to get up now?"

"Yes, of course, dear."

Nancy helped her to her feet and with one arm around the housekeeper's waist guided her gently to the blue brocaded sofa in the living room. "Now, you lie down here, Hannah, and if you can, tell me exactly what the man looked like."

"I'll never forget him!" Mrs. Gruen shuddered slightly as she settled herself on the sofa. "He was powerfully built and had a crooked nose, and one eyelid sort of drooped."

The squint-eyed thief from the River Heights Country Club! But how did he get into the house, and what was he looking for?

Nancy decided it was time to seek help from the police. She had already waited too long, it seemed, considering what had just happened to Hannah. She went to the phone and called Police Chief McGinnis. After reporting the whole story, beginning with her own clash with the crook, she added, "In light of his telephone threat, I feel this may be getting serious, Chief."

"You bet it's serious, when innocent citizens are attacked in their homes!" McGinnis growled. "I'll be there myself in ten minutes."

While she was waiting, Nancy went to the desk and sat down with pencil and paper to try and sketch the squint-eyed intruder. Being a talented artist, trained in life drawing, she soon achieved a good likeness.

"That's the man, Nancy!" Hannah exclaimed when she saw the drawing. "That's exactly how he looked!"

When Chief McGinnis arrived with two officers from the burglary squad, he also was highly approving. "This sketch will be a big help, Nancy. With this and his height and weight, we should have a good chance of identifying him. My men here will look for fingerprints or any other clues. Anything missing, by the way?"

"We haven't checked yet," said Nancy. "But it doesn't look as though he disturbed anything downstairs."

"We'll look around," McGinnis said comfortingly. "And perhaps you'll come with us. I'm sure your sharp eyes will be able to spot anything out of place."

Nancy insisted that Hannah continue resting on the sofa while she went through the house with the policemen. As it turned out, there were no signs that the crook had been upstairs at all.

"I'll put his picture and description on the police wire," Chief McGinnis promised before leaving. "If this creep's got any record at all, we should be able to get a 'make' from the FBI."

"Thank you, Chief," Nancy said gratefully. "I feel better already."

As Hannah had dinner all prepared, Nancy had only to put it in the oven and make a salad with the tomatoes Hannah had picked. She insisted that the housekeeper rest until Mr. Drew arrived home and dinner was served.

Later that evening, when the meal was over, she cleared off the dining room table and did the dishes, then went to the phone. She had made up her mind to call Simon Shand. A servant answered, but the trucking tycoon promptly came to the phone when he heard who was calling.

"Mr. Shand," said Nancy, "at the country club last Saturday, you asked me to try and catch that thief who was after Kim Vernon's golf bag. Would you care for a progress report?"

"You bet I would!" he rasped. "Say, you don't let any grass grow under your feet, do you? Why not come over and deliver your report in person."

"Very well," Nancy agreed. This might be a

chance, she hoped, to find out how, if at all, Simon Shand himself fitted into the mystery.

Shand gave her directions to his apartment, which turned out to be located in a large, luxurious modern high-rise recently erected in town, overlooking the riverfront.

"Well, well," he said, rubbing his hands together as she was shown into his window-walled living room, glossily furnished in ultramodern decor. "I'm really curious to hear what you've found out. Please sit down, Miss Drew."

Nancy told him about the squint-eyed crook's threatening phone call and went on to report his attack on Hannah Gruen that afternoon.

Shand was properly indignant. But he added with a frown, "What about clues, though? I mean, how're we gonna get a line on this guy? Where does all this leave us?"

"I don't know yet. But the police are now circulating his description, and they think there's a good chance he can be identified. Naturally that'll be a big help in tracking him down." Nancy hesitated, studying her host keenly. "Actually, I'm wondering whether *you* can't give me any help, Mr. Shand?"

"How do you mean?"

"I mean, are you being completely frank with

me? Call it feminine intuition, if you like," Nancy challenged, "but I still have a feeling you may have some personal motive for wanting this thief caught. Have you?"

"Look, I've already told you, I'm like every other private citizen these days—I'm fed up with crime in the streets. Here's a hood with gall enough to try and swipe something belonging to a famous sports star. In full view of a whole crowd of people, mind you, and right while she's being interviewed a few yards away! I think that kind of crook belongs behind bars—and, honey, I'm ready to pay you plenty to put him there! Does that answer your question?"

"Yes, thank you." Nancy smiled and nodded noncommittally. "One thing, Mr. Shand. The thief dropped a small red object, and then stopped just long enough to snatch it up."

"What about it?"

"I keep wondering what it was. Did you happen to catch a glimpse of it? It may sound very odd, but it looked like a *red spider!*"

Nancy was watching the trucking tycoon closely as she spoke. At her last words, Shand's face seemed to freeze—but not before Nancy caught a sudden startled look in his eyes.

But he merely shook his head in reply, although his expression seemed somewhat tight-lipped. "Nope. I do remember him stopping to pick up something, but I wasn't close enough to see what it was."

From that point on, Shand's manner became strained and uncomfortable, and conversation lagged. Nancy rose from her chair. "Well, I've made my report, so I'd better be going."

Shand stood up quickly and walked her to the door. "That's what I like, the way you keep plugging away on a case. Keep up the good work, girlie!"

One thing's certain, Nancy thought with a wry smile on her way down to the lobby in the elevator. Once I mentioned a red spider, he couldn't get rid of me fast enough!

The next morning was Saturday and the opening day of the Oceanview Festival. Nancy picked up Bess and George early and drove to the Footlighters' theater, where a big truck and two smaller ones were waiting to be loaded with scenery and sets. Everyone in the group was on hand, and the female members had called on their boyfriends or brothers or husbands to help.

Margo and Hamilton Spencer were everywhere at once, making sure that all props and other items were put aboard in proper order.

Finally everything was on the trucks, and the young people began piling into their waiting cars. Ned Nickerson and Dave Evans, a college pal who often dated Bess Marvin, climbed into the cab of the big truck, while other young men manned the two smaller ones. A holiday mood prevailed.

Oceanview was about an hour's ride from River Heights. The festival performances were to be held in a concrete amphitheater built on a hillside overlooking the town, with a splendid view of the sea.

As they drove through the pleasant shore community, they saw flags flying, banners advertising the festival, and bunting decorating the shops. The town was already thronged with visitors for the week-long celebration.

The Footlighters' little caravan turned right at the waterfront onto a road which led up the hill from the heart of town to the gleaming white amphitheater.

The Spencers led the procession to the back of the shell which enclosed the stage. Here, the trucks were backed up, one by one, to a loading dock to discharge the scenery and props, which were then whisked down by elevator to underground storerooms.

"Wow, what a setup! I just hope we learn our way around before Tuesday night," Bess fretted after a bit of hasty exploration. "This place is a maze, and the stage looks huge!"

"Don't worry," Nancy said soothingly. "I'm sure Mr. and Mrs. Spencer will have everything under control long before curtain time."

With everyone helping, the work was soon completed, and those of the group who had to return to River Heights began pulling out for home.

"The opera tonight will be *The Barber of Seville*," Nancy told her boyfriend. "I wish you and Dave could stay and see it."

"So do I," Ned replied. "But we have to get these trucks back by five o'clock. That doesn't mean we have to leave right away, though. Let's go get some hamburgers and shakes, and then check out the beach."

"Good idea," said George. "I'm starved!"

"Hey, that's my line!" said Bess in a shocked voice. "I thought you were the one who never got hungry?"

Everyone burst out laughing.

At about 3:30 that afternoon, the boys left for the return trip to River Heights. "See you tomorrow, Nancy!" Ned waved as he drove off.

Nancy herself had planned to go home that evening after the opera. But Bess and George prevailed on her to stay overnight at their motel.

"Sure I won't be crowding you?"

"Don't be silly," said George. "With accommodations so tight, everyone'll be doubling up. The more the merrier!"

Although at first they talked of enjoying a swim before dinner, the girls changed their minds and strolled back up the hill to the amphitheater. All three were fascinated by its vast size and were eager to look around leisurely, to familiarize themselves with its features, both above and below ground.

At this late hour of the afternoon, a sort of suspenseful hush seemed to have settled over the place, as if in anticipation of the excitement to come. Only a few people were prowling about backstage. The scenery was now in place for the opera, and one or two members of the orchestra were practicing in the pit. Otherwise the evening's performers seemed to be napping in their dressing rooms or to have gone off for an early meal.

Nancy, who had wandered away from her two companions, came upon a luxurious lounge with deep leather chairs and soft lights. At one end, a group was softly talking, while at the other, relaxing with a newspaper, sat Renzo Scaglia.

He looked up as Nancy opened the door, then leaped to his feet with a smile of recognition. "Ah, my dear Miss Drew! Welcome to the greenroom! Come in, do!"

"I'm just exploring this wonderful theater," Nancy explained. "I hope I'm not disturbing you."

"No, no, no. Not at all! For me, talking is relaxing, and that's what I'm doing now—relaxing before tonight's performance. I shall be singing the role of Count Almaviva, did you know?"

"Yes, I've seen the posters—and I'm looking forward to hearing you."

At Scaglia's insistence, she took a chair and prepared to chat for a while, feeling this might be an opportunity to gain some interesting information. "Haven't you forgotten something, Signor Scaglia?" she inquired, her lips twitching in a faint smile.

"Forgotten something? How do you mean, my dear?"

"When we met in River Heights, you challenged me to solve a crime that had once been committed here."

"Ah . . . that." The tenor looked slightly embarrassed, as if he wished he had never brought up the subject. "It is of no importance now, believe me—hardly worthy of your detective skill."

"Don't you at least care to tell me about it?"

"Another time, perhaps. Why waste these pleasant moments with talk of such matters?" Scaglia dismissed the subject with a smile and a graceful wave of his hand.

Nancy was puzzled, as well as a trifle disappointed. For some reason, the singer appeared to have decided it was better to let sleeping dogs lie. However, she might still pick up a few useful facts. "Tell me, Signor Scaglia—did you know Madame Arachne Onides well?"

The bearded singer glanced at her sharply, but replied after only an instant of hesitation. "Ah yes, I knew her very well indeed. She was—*is* unforgettable. What a voice, what fire, what verve! But alas, Arachne was also cruel, devious . . . even unscrupulous."

Once launched on the subject, Renzo Scaglia talked freely about the famous prima donna. Nancy was amazed at the things he told concerning her spendthrift ways, her greed, her stinginess, her generosity, her petty jealousy, her willingness to strike down anyone who stood in her way. But above all, he talked about her wonderful talent and her blazing ambition to become the world's greatest opera diva.

Nancy found it difficult, however, to make out Scaglia's own attitude toward Madame Arachne. At times he seemed to be sneering at her, at others his tone was adoring. The picture he painted added up to that of an intensely beautiful, gifted woman who was also a mass of contradictions.

"Dare I ask if you were in love with her?" Nancy said softly.

Scaglia heaved a sigh and looked soulfully at Nancy. "I can tell you this, my dear. When Arachne died in that devastating plane crash at sea, for me a light went out of the world—never again to see her or hear . . . !"

Suddenly the bearded tenor stiffened. His eyes looked past Nancy—at someone or something that plainly did not please Renzo Scaglia.

# 10

## A Sinister Symbol

Nancy turned, wondering who or what had caused Scaglia to react so strangely. She saw that a man had just entered the greenroom. Nancy recognized him at once.

He was the mustached, courtly-looking gentleman whom she had seen leaving Brett Hulme's workshop on Monday afternoon!

The recognition was mutual. "Well, well, well! What a pleasure!" the newcomer exclaimed. "We meet again, young lady!"

Nancy smiled back. "So we do!"

Today he was sportily dressed in a casual white Italian suit and open-necked silk sport shirt. But his mustache was as glossily waxed and twirled as before, and he was brandishing a bamboo cane in the same jaunty way that a British military officer carries his swagger stick. Though slender and youthful in bearing, the man appeared to be in his late fifties.

Scaglia looked perplexed. "You two know each other?"

"Only by sight," said Nancy, her blue eyes sparkling merrily. "We've never been formally introduced."

"Then kindly allow me to do so!" By now, Renzo Scaglia had regained his poise, his white teeth flashing in a brilliant smile. "This gentleman, my dear, is Mr. Eugene Horvath—whose late wife, Madame Arachne Onides, we were just discussing. And this attractive young lady, Gene, is the famous girl detective, Miss Nancy Drew!"

Nancy was astonished to learn that the newcomer was the widower of the much-headlined opera star. Horvath, for his part, seemed equally startled and impressed to meet Nancy Drew.

"How very unusual!" he exclaimed, staring at her more admiringly than ever. "I must confess, Miss Drew, I have never met either a police detective or a private eye before. But seeing one as lovely as you makes me feel I've been missing something all these years!"

Nancy found his flattery pleasant, but too obvious to raise a blush. "I doubt if I qualify as a private eye," she chuckled. "I'm strictly an amateur at detecting."

"My dear Miss Drew, you're entirely too modest!" Horvath protested. "I've read about the mysteries you've solved—at least the more sensational ones that have been reported in the papers. Keep on as you're going, and you may well end up on a par with Sherlock Holmes!"

Seeing the twinkle in his eyes, the young sleuth burst out laughing. But Scaglia said drily:

"Watch out, Nancy, or you're more likely to end up as the latest celebrity in Gene's menagerie! I should have warned you: he makes a hobby of 'collecting' famous people."

With a tinge of malice, the tenor added, "In fact I sometimes think that's how he came to marry Arachne."

If Horvath was offended by this remark, he gave no sign. Instead he inquired good-naturedly, "Are you here in Oceanview for festival week, Miss Drew? . . . or may I call you Nancy?"

"Please do," the teenager replied gracefully. "No, I'll be going home tomorrow. But I do hope to come back later and see more of the festival events—besides tonight's opera, I mean."

"If you two will excuse me," Renzo Scaglia cut

in coldly, "I really must be getting back to my dressing room, to begin warming up for this evening's performance."

With a stiff little bow, he turned and strode out of the greenroom. Nancy knew that he was irritated by Eugene Horvath's arrival. But she could not tell if this was merely due to a star's egotistical annoyance at no longer being the center of attention, or what seemed more likely, whether he actively, and perhaps jealously, disliked Horvath.

"A very great tenor!" the latter remarked after he had gone. "One of the greatest since Enrico Caruso—perhaps *the* greatest. My adored Arachne was *very* fond of him. And he of her."

With a wry smile, Horvath went on, "Indeed, I sometimes wonder if Renzo has ever forgiven me for marrying her. But enough of all that! Let us go outside, my dear, and see what is happening on stage."

From the way he walked freely about the amphitheater and exchanged joking remarks with people they passed, Horvath seemed to be a well-known festival personage. Nancy assumed this was because he was the widower of Madame Arachne.

The hum of activity had increased. Stagehands were busy adjusting lights and scenery inside the festival shell. Onstage, a television reporter was now interviewing one of the festival officials.

"Did you come to Oceanview alone, Nancy?" Horvath inquired.

"No, with some friends," she replied. "We belong to a little theater group from River Heights called the Footlighters. They're to do a play here on Tuesday."

"Ah! Then you're also a budding actress?"

"Only an understudy," Nancy twinkled.

"In that case, tell your director he's overlooking a great possibility!"

"It's kind of you to say so, but I prefer detecting." Changing the subject, Nancy said hesitantly, "Mr. Horvath, I know how you must have grieved when you lost your wife. Do you mind talking about her?"

"Of course not, my dear. There's no one I'd rather talk about than Arachne. What would you like to know?"

"How did the two of you happen to meet and marry?"

Horvath explained that he had long been an admirer of the famous diva and had been thrilled to meet her at a dinner party in New York. Having been told by their hostess that he was a retired, wealthy businessman, Arachne asked his advice about certain investments.

Later, Horvath related, he became her business manager and eventually, as their relationship grew closer, she accepted his proposal of marriage.

"We had only a year of happiness together before her tragic plane accident"—Horvath sighed deeply—"but I am the luckiest man in the world to have had such a wife as Arachne for even that long. I shall cherish her memory always!"

His fond recollection and description of Madame Arachne, thought Nancy, certainly differed from Renzo Scaglia's!

As they went on chatting, she asked if he remembered Maggie Farr.

"Arachne's former dresser? Of course!" Horvath responded. "Do you know her?"

"We met recently. I'm sorry to say she's now in the hospital, suffering from a stroke." Nancy explained that Mrs. Farr had lost her power of speech, but had tried to communicate something about a spider, which in turn seemed to relate in some way to her former mistress, Madame Arachne. "Do you have any idea what she might be talking about?"

"Not the slightest." Horvath looked surprised and puzzled. "It sounds rather weird. Are you sure her mind hasn't been affected?"

"I don't think so. At least her doctor hasn't suggested any such thing." Privately Nancy was taken aback by his suggestion. Was it possible that Maggie might be hallucinating, or having delusions which caused her to lose touch with reality?

But no! Nancy rejected the notion at once. The very coincidences relating Maggie's cryptic message to Kim Vernon, a spiderlike object, and Madame Arachne—coincidences which at first had seemed too great to accept—were also too great to be brushed aside as mere whimsical ravings.

However, the mention of the spider had reminded Nancy of someone else. "By the way, do you know if your wife was acquainted with Brett Hulme?" she asked casually.

"Oh yes, indeed," Horvath nodded. "One might almost say Brett was a protégé of hers. Arachne helped launch his career, you see. When he first opened his design studio, she introduced him to many celebrities who later wore his creations and thus made his work famous. And she also used her influence to get his designs exhibited in museums and galleries."

108

Nancy's conversation with the late opera star's husband was interrupted as she caught sight of Bess and George. They had just come up from the complex of rooms and passageways below stage.

When her two friends waved to Nancy, she beckoned them over and introduced them to Eugene Horvath. Bess dimpled excitedly as he took their hands in turn and gave each a little bow. She was obviously bowled over by his elegant style of dress and urbane, courtly manner.

"You must all come out to my island estate sometime during the festival," remarked Horvath, beaming at the three pretty girls.

"You live on an island?" asked Bess, wide-eyed.

"My very own, not too far offshore. My chauffeur will come and pick you up and drive you to the boat landing, then bring you out to the island in my motor cruiser."

"Isn't he *charming*!" gushed Bess after they had parted from Horvath and he had gone over to speak to the conductor of the orchestra.

"Cool it," teased George. "He hasn't proposed yet—remember, he's still in mourning for Madame Arachne!"

That night, the girls thoroughly enjoyed *The Barber of Seville* as performed by the festival opera company, and next morning they went swimming off Oceanview's splendid white sandy beach.

Much to her friends' regret, however, Nancy insisted on driving back to River Heights on Sunday afternoon. She was keenly determined to pursue her investigation of the mystery.

As soon as she got home, Nancy telephoned Buzz Hammond, the golf pro at the River Heights Country Club, to ask him for the address and phone number of the riverside cottage where Kim Vernon was staying. In light of her emotional outburst when questioned about Madame Arachne or a spider, Nancy hoped the golf star might now be willing to talk more freely.

Kim agreed to see Nancy early Monday afternoon. The two girls sat in chintz-covered, deep-cushioned chairs in the cheerful living room of the cottage.

Kim's manner was calm and pleasant. However, she seemed no more inclined than she had before to discuss the reasons for her withdrawal from the Charleston Cup match. "Let's just say I felt I needed a rest from competition," she told Nancy.

"May I ask a more personal question?"

Kim chuckled. "No harm in asking. That's not saying I'll answer it."

"Why did you pick River Heights as a place to stay?" said Nancy.

Kin shrugged. "As I told you, I've always liked this town. It's near my brother in Bradley. And of course being offered the use of this cottage also had a lot to do with it."

"Did the fact that Brett Hulme lives near here also have anything to do with it?"

The black-haired golf star seemed to wince slightly, and blushed. "I . . . I certainly wouldn't object to seeing him again . . . if that's what you're getting at."

Nancy thought this a rather unusual way of answering her question—and perhaps more revealing than Kim had intended. The teenage sleuth had the same feeling she had sensed in talking to Brett: that very likely Kim, too, now regretted the breakup of their romance, just as he did.

"Do you and Brett have any plans to see each other?" Nancy probed.

Kim Vernon shook her head and smiled—a bit wistfully, Nancy thought. "No, I just want to keep my hand in at golf, but otherwise relax. Maybe find time for a bit of swimming, boating, tennis . . ."

As the doorbell rang, she broke off to glance out the window, then rose from her chair. "In fact, I ordered a racket Saturday afternoon. That's probably the delivery man from the store!"

Kim answered the bell, accepted something from the man who rang, then closed the door and eagerly began to unwrap the package. From its shape, it appeared to be the tennis racket she was expecting.

But a moment later, Kim gasped in horror and flung the racket aside! Covering her face with her hands, she sank into a chair and burst into shuddering sobs.

Nancy picked up the racket, her own eyes widening as she did so.

Instead of normal racket webbing, it was strung with glistening threads that formed a *cobweb design!*

# *11*

## *Trapped!*

Cobwebs and spiders!

Obviously, Nancy realized, the weirdly strung racket must be connected in some way to the strange mystery that seemed to be blighting Kim Vernon's career. But how? And what did it mean?

The black-haired golf star seemed like an innocent victim who had become entangled in a spiderweb of trouble and danger!

Whatever the answer, this cobwebbed racket might be the clue Nancy had been hoping for, the clue that would help her unravel the mystery!

Should she press Kim for information while she was emotionally upset and her guard was down?

A hasty glance at the hysterically sobbing young woman was all Nancy needed to decide against this course of action. The thought of taking advantage of Kim's distraught condition to worm information out of her was too distasteful.

Dropping the tennis racket, Nancy snatched up her shoulder bag and darted toward the door. "I'm going after that delivery man!" she cried.

As the teenage sleuth burst out of the cottage, she saw him just driving away.

*He's a phony!* thought Nancy. Not only was he wearing no uniform cap or jacket, but instead of a delivery van, he was driving an unmarked brown sedan!

Sliding swiftly behind the wheel of her blue sports car, Nancy keyed the engine to life and took off with a vroom of exhaust. As she sped in pursuit, she saw the brown car turning off the riverfront road, some distance ahead.

Nancy followed. In broad daylight, there was little or nothing she could do to conceal the fact that she was tailing the brown car. Luckily its driver seemed unaware that he was being followed—which at least kept the pursuit from turning into a high-speed chase!

The mystery man soon left behind the pleasant, tree-shaded suburban area of riverside bungalows and cottages. His car was heading toward the heart of town.

As she kept it in sight, Nancy was turning the racket riddle over and over in her mind.

Russ Chaffee had told her how upset Kim had become on two earlier occasions—once on receiving a drawing of a red spider, and another time when someone sent her an actual living specimen. The delivery of the cobwebbed tennis racket looked like the latest move in a deliberate campaign of terror!

Was it some similar incident that had led to Kim's withdrawal from the Charleston Cup match?

But if so, who was going to such lengths to frighten her?—and why?

Did spiders and cobwebs remind her of some terrifying experience in the past? Somehow, to Nancy's finely tuned sleuthing instincts, the whole situation smacked strongly of blackmail.

In any event, the man in the brown car must be in on the plot. And Nancy was determined to find out what lay behind it!

As they reached a busy, workaday section of River Heights, traffic increased. Nancy was able to drop behind one or more other cars, yet still keep the brown sedan in view.

They were now entering a run-down area of small factories and aging commercial buildings, many of them empty and vandalized. The brown car was a block ahead when Nancy saw it swing suddenly into a driveway on the right.

Crossing the intersection, she pulled over to the curb, jumped out, and quietly followed on foot.

The driveway, Nancy now saw, led to an old warehouse—deserted, judging by the look of it. The brown sedan was parked in the cindered yard in front of the building, but its driver was no longer in sight. Evidently he had gone into the warehouse.

Nancy approached it cautiously. The wooden door opened to her touch. Entering, she stopped to look around and get her bearings. The vast, dusty room was unpleasantly dark and gloomy. The only light came in through two dirty windows, high up on the front wall, on either side of the doorway.

"Now where has he gone to?" Nancy said to herself. There was no sound.

The young sleuth took a small flashlight out of her bag and switched it on. In one corner she could see some pipes and wooden poles and

116

cardboard boxes. Otherwise the room seemed empty. The whole place smelled musty and un-aired.

Aiming her flashlight downward, she played its beam back and forth over the floor. Nancy stifled a gasp as the yellow cone of light revealed foot-prints in the dust!

What luck! she thought and began following them. They tracked toward a door on the right, which Nancy had failed to see when she shone her beam about the room.

The door stood slightly ajar. Slowly and gently Nancy pushed it open. Beyond lay a dark pas-sage. Nancy tiptoed through the doorway to see where the passage led—and a moment later wished she hadn't!

Someone grabbed her from behind and hit her on the back of the head!

With a faint groan, Nancy sank to the floor unconscious.

How many minutes or hours she may have lain there, the teenage detective had no way of know-ing when at last she began to revive. Gradually her eyes fluttered open. Another soft moan es-caped her lips as she discovered the full extent of her plight.

Her wrists were tied behind her back—her ankles bound together—and a gag tied tightly across her mouth!

Oh, what a mess! thought Nancy. And I walked right into it with my eyes wide open!

Obviously the man in the brown sedan must have known all along he was being followed. And once having spotted her in his rearview mirror, he cunningly lured her into a trap!

To make matters worse, her head ached slightly. But there was no point in dwelling on her troubles, Nancy realized. The important thing now was to find a way out of her predicament!

Suddenly she became aware of a glow of light along the floor. Nancy had only to roll her eyes to see where it was coming from.

Her flashlight lay where it had fallen! And it was still burning! So evidently she hadn't been unconscious as long as she feared.

By turning her head, Nancy could see her bag a short distance away from where she was lying. By rolling and twisting, she got close enough to reach it and pry open the clasp behind her back.

Slowly she fumbled through the bag's contents until she found her nail file. Then Nancy began the tedious process of trying to file and saw through the cords around her wrists.

It was slow, clumsy work. And painful as well. But finally, stiff and perspiring, she had her hands free. Oh, how good it felt to stretch!

Nancy sighed, took off her gag, and rested for a few minutes. Then she started untying the rope binding her ankles. At last, free of all her bonds, she retrieved her flashlight and shoulder bag and stood up—almost faint with eagerness to get out in the open air and sunshine again.

"No need to be quiet now!" Nancy told herself. Returning from the passageway to the main room, she hurried across the dusty floor toward the door by which she had entered the warehouse. But this time, as she turned the handle, it refused to open.

*She was locked in!*

"Oh, no," Nancy muttered in dismay. She went back to the passageway and followed it to the rear of the building. It led to a garage area and a large shuttered door which evidently opened on to a loading dock at the back. But here, too, everything was securely locked.

Heart thumping anxiously, Nancy retraced her steps to the main room. Only a squeaky noise at her feet warned her in time to avoid treading on a rat that darted across her path. Her skin crawled at the thought!

The only possible way out seemed to be the pair of dirty windows. But they were much too high up to reach.

Nancy screamed for help and pounded on the street door. But there was no response. The warehouse was in such a deserted area it would be a miracle if any passerby heard her!

Nancy's heart sank as she realized that it might be a long time until she was found. Before help arrived, she could starve to death—or even, she reflected with a terrified shudder, fall victim to the building's hungry rats!

# *12*

## *Library Clue*

As she stood in the warehouse fighting despair, Nancy stared at the dust-specked beam of sunlight slanting down from one of the high windows.

Suddenly she snapped her fingers. She had just remembered seeing a fire detector on the far side wall when she made her first inspection of the warehouse interior.

Groping in her bag, Nancy pulled out a small magnifying glass and a pad of notepaper. She tore off a piece, then held the glass so as to focus the sunbeam into a concentrated pinpoint of light and heat.

As soon as the paper began to smolder and burn, Nancy hurried over and held it up as close as she could to the fire detector. Almost at once the device actuated an alarm bell!

Nancy dropped the burning paper and stamped it out, praying that the alarm would also register at the nearest fire station, or else that someone would report it.

Within minutes, the clanging bells and wailing sirens of fire engines could be heard coming closer. Soon they halted just outside.

Taking her flashlight, Nancy threw it up at one of the windows as hard as she could. With a crash, the glass shattered and Nancy began to yell.

"Hey, what's going on! Who's in there?" a fireman bellowed.

"I'm locked in!" Nancy cried.

In seconds, the door was smashed open and Nancy dashed out into the sunshine. The firemen listened sympathetically to her story, impressed with her ingenious method of escape.

Almost as if in response to her next thought, a patrol car pulled up to the curb. Nancy recognized one of the policemen in it as Officer Morgan, whom she had met before.

She quickly repeated her story to them while the fire trucks pulled away.

"What did this fake delivery man look like?" asked Officer Morgan's partner.

Nancy shrugged regretfully. "Sorry, but I never did get a good look at his face."

However, she described the brown sedan and gave the police its license number.

"This may do the trick," said Officer Morgan, taking down the information. "I'll radio word to headquarters right away!"

"Incidentally," Nancy asked his partner as Morgan got into the police car again, "do you happen to know who owns this building?"

The officer frowned and scratched his forehead. "Well, I believe it used to be occupied by Shand Trucking Company. But it's been empty for some time now, so I don't know whether they still own it or not."

Nancy mused as she drove home. Once again, it seemed, Simon Shand had entered the picture. On the other hand, the fact that the phony delivery man had used the warehouse as a trap did not necessarily prove that Shand himself was involved. Assuming the driver was a professional crook, once he sensed he was being tailed, he might simply have picked out an obviously empty building and used a picklock or skeleton key to gain entry and set a trap for his pursuer.

As soon as she arrived home, Nancy called directory assistance and requested the number of

Jack Vernon's campaign office in Bradley. Then she dialed the number.

A woman campaign worker answered. She explained that the candidate was away from his office, keeping several speaking dates. However, at Nancy's urgent request, she gave the teenager a tentative appointment to see him the following afternoon. "Mind you, I can't promise Mr. Vernon will talk to you," the woman cautioned. "He has an awfully busy schedule just now."

"Please tell him it's very important," said Nancy and hung up before the woman could make any further excuses.

Shortly before dinner that evening, Police Chief McGinnis telephoned. He reported that the brown sedan had been found abandoned in the street. "But it was a stolen car," he added, "so finding it doesn't help much."

Nor had Kim Vernon been very helpful or cooperative. She claimed to have paid little or no attention to the delivery man's appearance, and said she had hurled the frightening cobweb racket far out into the river. But she declined to say why it had upset her so much.

"Any luck yet, in identifying that squint-eyed thief with the broken nose?" Nancy inquired.

"Not so far. But we'll keep trying."

Nancy's appointment with Jack Vernon was for three o'clock on Tuesday afternoon. The budding politician had set up his campaign headquarters in an office above a shop in Bradley.

"A pleasure to see you again, Nancy," he said, rising to greet her.

Nancy quickly told him of Kim's hysterical reaction to the cobwebbed racket, and her own narrow escape after following the mystery man who had delivered it.

"So you see," she concluded, "your sister may be in danger. Frankly, if you know anything that might help, I think it's your duty to talk."

The tall, dark-haired young political candidate was clearly upset by the news. After pacing about the office for a few moments, he nodded anxiously. "All right. But we can't talk here."

As he spoke, he shot a worried glance at the outer office, scarcely larger than the one they were in, where several volunteers were stuffing envelopes with brochures for his mail campaign.

"Where would you suggest?" said Nancy.

Vernon pulled thoughtfully on his lower lip. "Tell you what. If you could meet me in Riverside Park tomorrow night, sometime between seven-thirty and eight, we could sit and talk. I'll be waiting just inside the Park Drive entrance."

"Good. I'll be there." After thanking him and promising to keep anything he told her in strictest confidence, Nancy left Jack Vernon's office.

She planned to eat an early dinner before starting for Oceanview to witness the Footlighters' performance of *A Scream in the Dark* at the festival that evening. But after a quick glance at her watch, Nancy decided she would have time to stop off at the public library on her way home.

Parking outside the red brick building, Nancy went in and began looking through the reference volumes that listed magazine articles several years back. Tonight she might be seeing Renzo Scaglia and Eugene Horvath again, so she thought it might be useful to find out more about Madame Arachne Onides.

Soon she was seated at a table in a quiet alcove with a number of magazines containing pieces about the famous prima donna. Suddenly, turning the page of one magazine, Nancy caught her breath. There, in full color, was a close-up photograph of Madame Arachne, and pinned to the front of her gown was a magnificent red gemstone ornament—*an ornament that resembled a jeweled spider!*

# 13

## Moonlight Island

Once again Nancy made use of her small magnifying glass. Holding it over the magazine photo, she stared in awe at the jeweled spider.

It appeared to have been crafted from two smooth pigeon's-blood rubies. The gems, one smaller than the other, were bound together in a silvery figure-8 setting to form the spider's body. Its eight long legs were crusted with tiny sparkling diamonds.

*How beautiful!* was Nancy's first reaction. Her second was, it must have cost a fortune!

Lowering the magnifying glass, she read the caption below the picture:

> *Proud of her Greek heritage, Madame Onides had this magnificent ruby brooch designed to symbolize her own name. In classic Greek myth,*

*Arachne was a beautiful maiden whom the God-*
*dess Athena transformed into a spider. Shortly*
*before this article went to press, the brooch, valued*
*at almost half a million dollars, was stolen from*
*the opera star's dressing room during a perform-*
*ance at the Oceanview Festival.*

Nancy gasped. *A theft at the Oceanview Festival!*
Could this have been the crime which Renzo
Scaglia had challenged her to solve?

Nancy eagerly perused the rest of the
magazine article, but could find no further mention of the ruby brooch or the robbery. Nor did
any of the other pieces about Madame Arachne
cover this subject.

With a sigh, Nancy closed the last of the
magazines she had brought to the table and
glanced at her wristwatch. To her dismay, it was
4:57!

If I don't hurry, I'll be late for the play! she
chided herself.

Gathering up the magazines, she turned them
in at the desk, then hurried out to her car.

Hannah Gruen emerged from the kitchen,
wiping her hands on her apron as Nancy came
rushing into the house. Seeing the teenager's expression, the motherly woman said, "You'll have
time for some of my meat pie and apple tart,
won't you?"

"Oh, Hannah dear, I don't think so," Nancy cried, "I stopped in the library and I forgot to keep an eye on the clock. I'm afraid I'm going to have to dress and run!"

Scampering upstairs, Nancy showered and changed into an ivory-colored silk dress. After a quick touch of comb and brush to her hair, she crammed some toilet articles, nightwear, a change of clothes, and her bathing suit into an overnight bag and hurried down to the front hall, where Hannah Gruen was waiting.

"Sure you haven't time for a bite, dear?"

"I wish I could, but I seem to be running later than ever," Nancy replied with an apologetic smile.

"Just don't take any chances—please!" the housekeeper begged.

"I promise!" Nancy gave her a quick hug and went flying out the door.

Fortunately, traffic on the freeway thinned out considerably during the dinner hour. Nancy made such good time that, as she neared Ocean-view, she was able to stop at a diner for a hamburger, French fries, and a milkshake.

By doing so, it turned out that she had also avoided the worst jam of cars crawling bumper-to-bumper up the hill to the festival amphitheater. Luckily a few empty spaces were still left as Nancy pulled into the parking area.

By the time she reached their dressing rooms, the Footlighters were almost ready to go on stage. Nancy, who had chosen a dress suitable for her understudy role and would only require makeup, apologized for her lateness to the Spencers. "Do you think you'll need me tonight?"

"Doesn't look that way, darling," said Margo, "but it's still a comfort to know you're here."

Standing in the wings, Nancy and George whispered encouragement to Bess, who looked a bit pale and nervous with last-minute butterflies. Presently the house lights dimmed and the curtain rose on *A Scream in the Dark.*

The audience was soon gripped by the suspenseful yet amusing melodrama. Hamilton Spencer played an irritable author of mystery thrillers who had come to a holiday resort for a restful weekend, only to find himself stumbling into trouble at every turn. Bess played his harried secretary.

Laughs and startled gasps punctuated every scene, and the first act ended to tumultuous applause.

During the intermission, Nancy stayed in the wings with the stagehands while George accompanied Bess and the others down to the dressing rooms.

"*Buona sera, mia cara* Nancy!" said a familiar voice. The pretty sleuth turned and saw the smiling, bearded face of Renzo Scaglia.

"How nice to see you again, Signor Scaglia," she smiled back.

"The pleasure is mine, I assure you! This has turned into a most rewarding evening. Your play is certainly pleasing the audience—though I am sure the performance would be even more enjoyable were you in the cast!"

"Thanks, but they seem to be doing very well without me," Nancy twinkled. "Anyhow, I've been too busy detecting."

"Indeed? And what sort of a mystery case are you working on now?"

"It may be connected with that mystery you challenged me to solve," said Nancy, then added: "I mean the theft of Madame Arachne's jeweled spider while she was singing here at Oceanview."

The tenor's olive-skinned face seemed to turn a shade paler.

"You are indeed a gifted sleuth, *signorina*," he murmured. "Almost uncannily so."

"Then I'm right that that was the unsolved crime you were referring to?"

132

"Scaglia nodded reluctantly. "*Si,* you are correct. Of course the challenge was foolish and unfair on my part. Obviously there is no possible way you could trace the thief after all this time." With a captivating smile he added, "So I hope you will forgive me and forget the whole matter!"

Nancy's sapphire eyes, however, did not wave from his gaze. "I'm not at all convinced it's impossible to solve," she said coolly, "though of course that depends on many things . . . such as your willingness to tell me exactly what happened. The theft occurred during a performance of *Carmen,* did it not?—and that night you were singing the role of Don José."

Renzo Scaglia looked around uncomfortably, as if he wished there were some way to cut short their conversation. "*Si,* that is so," he admitted with a sigh. "The robbery occurred during Act II. When Arachne returned to her dressing room and found out her priceless brooch had been stolen, she insisted on calling the police even though we were in the middle of the opera. The whole theater was in an uproar. The performance was ruined, of course. Though I must say, with all the excitement, I doubt that the audience felt cheated!"

The tenor laughed and flung out his hands in a

helpless shrugging gesture. "So there you have the whole story. What more can I tell you?"

Peeking out between the curtains for a moment, Scaglia added, "Your audience is returning, I see. Ah, and here come the actors from their dressing rooms! Time for me to leave, I think. *Ciao*, Nancy!"

The tenor's attitude puzzled the young detective. When Scaglia had first mentioned the crime back at the Footlighters' barn theater, he sounded eager to have the case reopened. But from the moment Nancy showed interest in probing the mystery, he seemed to draw back and become reluctant to discuss the matter.

The last act of the play scored an even bigger hit with the audience than the first half of the play. Loud handclapping and cheers filled the amphitheater as the final curtain came down and as the cast took repeated bows.

Nancy accompanied them down to the suite of dressing rooms below the stage level, where a happy celebration began. Numerous bouquets had been delivered, including a large cluster of gardenias and carnations for Bess.

"Oh, my goodness. They're from Mr. Horvath," Madame Arachne's husband!" Bess gasped, blushing with pleasure. "And he's inviting all three of us out to Moonlight Island as his overnight guests! Isn't that a romantic name for it, by the way?"

George and Nancy eagerly read the card which Bess handed them. It bore Eugene Horvath's signature boldly inscribed in purple ink, and said that he would send his manservant, Sandor, to pick up the girls, as he promised when they had met.

He added that he had hired a maid especially for this evening, to look after his hoped-for guests, and by accepting his invitation, they would make an elderly gentleman very happy.

Bess was thrilled at the chance to visit the glamorous island hideaway where Madame Arachne and her husband had spent their brief but happy marriage. Nancy felt this might be a chance to discover some valuable clue to the mystery surrounding the late opera star. George, adventurous as always, was more than willing to go along.

Minutes later, Sandor, the chauffeur-valet, knocked on the dressing room door. He was a strongly built, stony-faced man in a smart powder blue cap and uniform, but so silent that Nancy almost wondered at first if he were a mute.

At the wheel of Horvath's big, shiny dark limousine, he whisked the girls first to Bess and George's motel, then down to the boat landing where a luxurious motor cruiser was berthed and waiting. Soon they were cruising out over the moonlit waters of the bay toward their host's island estate. As they neared their destination, Sandor radioed ahead to announce their arrival.

The island loomed out of the sea, looking every bit as romantic as Bess could have wished. Rock-walled and roughly crescent-shaped, it was dotted with beautiful oaks and evergreens. In their midst, shimmering in the moonglow, rose Horvath's lovely white marble home, fronted by classical columns.

"Oh, isn't it lovely!" murmured Bess. "It looks like a Greek temple on a headland!"

The little cove formed by the island's crescent shape made a small natural harbor. Eugene Horvath himself was standing on the dock, waiting to greet them. "I cannot tell you how delighted I am that you have accepted my invitation!" he said, beaming at the three girls.

Golf carts had been provided to carry the guests up to the mansion. Here they met the stout, middle-aged maid, Elena, whom Horvath had hired for the girls' benefit that evening.

Over a delicious supper of cold chicken and salad, topped off by strawberries and ice cream, their host told Bess how much he had liked her performance in the play.

"We didn't even know you were there!" she said.

"Indeed I was, my dear, and enjoying every minute of it! But I watched from a private box and left before the final curtain came down."

When the meal was over, Mr. Horvath showed the girls around his mansion. It was filled with pictures and other mementos of his wife— including a marble bust of Madame Arachne.

He also took the girls into a small projection room, which looked like a tiny movie theater, and ran films of her outstanding operatic performances. The sheer dramatic power and color of the great diva's voice made Nancy shiver with excitement.

Later, while Bess and George were poring over some of Madame Arachne's colorful keepsakes, Eugene Horvath drew Nancy aside. "I must confess that I had another reason for inviting you and your friends out to the island," he told the young sleuth confidentially. "My life has been threatened! In fact that is why I tried to avoid being seen too publicly at the theater tonight."

He related that he had received several menacing phone calls from a man named Sweeney Flint. The caller warned him not to discuss his late wife's business affairs with anyone.

"Have you any idea who this Sweeney Flint might be?" Nancy asked.

Horvath shook his head gloomily. "The name means nothing to me. I wondered if you might have heard it during your detective work."

"Not until now," she replied. "But I'll certainly check him out with the police. He may have a criminal record. Was there any particular subject he warned you not to talk about?"

"No, 'business affairs' was the only term he used—and of course that could include almost any aspect of my wife's career."

"By the way," Nancy went on, "the last time we met, I told you your wife's former dresser, Maggie Farr, was trying to communicate something about a spider that concerned your wife. I think I know now what she was referring to."

"Indeed? And what is that?"

"A precious jeweled brooch in the shape of a spider. It was stolen from your wife's dressing room during an opera at the Oceanview Festival three years ago."

"Aaaah, yes!" A look of dawning comprehen-

138

sion came over Eugene Horvath's face. "Now that you tell me, I do recall Arachne mentioning a robbery of some sort. That was when we first met, before I became her business manager. But I never knew exactly what was stolen . . . A jeweled spider, you say? . . . Hmm, sounds most unusual."

It was well after midnight when the evening finally ended. The maid Elena showed the girls upstairs to their rooms. Bess and George, were to share a double room, while Nancy was given a smaller bedroom adjoining theirs.

It had been a long day. The girl detective's eyes closed and she drifted off to sleep almost as soon as her head touched the pillow.

Some time later, Nancy awoke with a sense of shock. An alarm bell was ringing, and someone was shouting. Flinging on a robe, she dashed out of the room.

At the other end of the corridor, she could hear Horvath's voice crying out, *"Help! . . . Help me!"*

# 14

## The Mysterious Intruder

The door next to Nancy's room opened, and George and Bess peered out anxiously, both pulling on robes. "What's going on?" George exclaimed.

Even as she spoke, another cry for help sounded from Eugene Horvath's room down the hall!

"I don't know, but I intend to find out!" Nancy declared.

Snatching up a slender metal figurine from its display stand to use as a makeshift weapon, Nancy dashed through the corridor toward their host's room. She rapped loudly on the door.

"Mr. Horvath! Are you all right?" she called. "Y-Y-Yes! . . . One moment, please!" In a few seconds, the mustached businessman looked out at Nancy, followed by her two friends. He was hastily belting a robe over his striped silk pajamas, and his usually suave face looked pale and haggard.

"What happened?" Nancy inquired.

"Someone attempted to climb into my room," Horvath replied, gesturing toward a pair of French windows which opened on to a balcony. "Because of those menacing phone calls I told you about, I recently had a security system installed. When the intruder climbed over the balcony rail, he tripped the burglar alarm!"

"Did he try to attack you, Mr. Horvath?" put in Bess Marvin, her plump face wide-eyed with fright.

"No, thank heavens—though I'm sure he intended to! He lingered on the balcony for a while, trying to make up his mind what to do, but the alarm bell and my calls for help finally frightened him off." Their host heaved a gusty sigh of relief. He now seemed to be recovering his poise, and his color was returning.

"Did you get a good look at him?" asked Nancy.

"I'm afraid not," Horvath confessed a bit sheepishly. "Besides the fact that I was upset, the

141

fellow had his back to the moonlight, so all I could see, really, was this dark form." He dabbed perspiration from his brow with a silk handkerchief.

"Should we search for him or call the police?" Nancy went on.

Horvath gave a nervous shudder. "There is no need for us to search. Sandor will have heard the alarm, just as you girls did. He is a trained bodyguard, by the way. He is probably out searching the grounds at this very moment!"

Half an hour later, while the group waited in the downstairs sitting room, sipping hot chocolate served by Elena, the chauffeur returned to report.

Sandor told Mr. Horvath that the intruder had been lurking in a clump of trees and had struck him from behind. "I managed to grab his leg as I went down, but he kicked me away and ran toward the dock."

"Did he have a boat?" asked George.

"A sports minisub," the chauffeur replied. "He got aboard and submerged before I could reach the motor cruiser."

"What about his appearance?" said Nancy. "Could you see his face?"

Sandor nodded grimly. "Well enough to remember it if I ever see him again! He had a big crooked nose, and there was something wrong with the left side of his face. I mean it was clenched up, as if he couldn't see properly on that side."

*The squint-eyed thief again!* Could he also be the threatening caller, Sweeney Flint? If so, Nancy realized, the name might provide an important lead in tracking him down.

All three girls slept late the next morning, due to their interrupted night's rest. After a swim in the tiny cove and a hearty breakfast, they returned to the mainland aboard Horvath's motor cruiser, with Sandor at the wheel. Their host came along for the brief trip and delivered the girls in his limousine to the amphitheater parking lot, where Nancy had left her blue sports car overnight.

Sandor transferred their luggage to Nancy's car, and the girls made their farewells to the suave, charming Eugene Horvath.

"You must all come and visit me again!" he said with a wave as his limousine moved off.

After dropping George and Bess at their homes, Nancy drove to her house. Her thoughts were filled with the puzzling pieces of the mystery.

"Oh, Hannah, it's good to be home again!" she cried as the housekeeper opened the screen door.

"I hope that doesn't mean you had a bad time?" Hannah said, greeting Nancy with a hug.

"Oh, no. The play was a big hit. And afterward, George and Bess and I were invited out to a beautiful island with a luxurious house on it. It belonged to Madame Arachne Onides, but now her husband lives there with just a servant."

"Oh, my!" Hannah exclaimed. "You'll have to tell me all about it over lunch."

"Golly, I'm sorry. We stopped to eat on our way home. But I'll sit and have a cup of tea while you eat lunch," Nancy said.

While Hannah ate and Nancy sipped her tea, she described the exciting events that had taken place on the island last night.

"Oh, my goodness, Nancy, that sounds dangerous," Hannah fretted.

"It just means I have another mystery to solve. Who's threatening Mr. Horvath and why?" Nancy paused and smiled. "But now you can understand how good it is to be home. It's so peaceful here!"

Later, as she helped Hannah clear the table,

144

Nancy said, "I'm going to pay Brett Hulme a visit this afternoon."

After unpacking her overnight bag, Nancy brushed her hair and freshened up, then set out to question the young jewelry designer. She felt sure he was the designer of the beautiful spider ornament stolen from Madame Onides.

As Nancy turned up the gravel drive to Brett Hulme's workshop, she saw him come out the door carrying an attaché case. He was dressed in a dark business suit, white shirt, and tie. Depositing the case in his own car, he turned to greet his visitor pleasantly.

"I'm sorry, Nancy, but as you see, I must leave. I have a number of appointments this afternoon. And also I'm delivering several orders."

"This won't take long," Nancy smiled.

"In that case, would you like to come inside?"

"Oh no, why don't we talk here?" Nancy pointed to some white painted garden chairs set out near a flower bed.

When Nancy told him about the ruby-and-diamond spider brooch that had been stolen from Madame Onides and asked if he had designed it, Brett's lips tightened.

"I'm sorry. I don't like to seem stubborn, but

that's something I'd rather not discuss with you."

"I'm also wondering if there's any connection between the jeweled spider and that beautiful silver cobweb necklace I saw you working on," she persisted.

"That necklace was commissioned by someone who has since canceled the order. I just don't feel free, Nancy, to tell you any more than that. And, no, I cannot reveal who my customer was," Brett ended on a note of finality.

Realizing that any further questions would be useless, Nancy stood up. "I'm sorry too, Brett. I think you'd really be helping Kim if you told me, but . . . if that's how you feel, I shan't keep you any longer."

With a smile and a wave, Nancy got into her car and turned back down the drive. In her rearview mirror, she could see Brett Hulme standing and watching her drive away. His expression looked anything but happy.

That night after dinner, Nancy set out to keep her rendezvous with Jack Vernon. The evening had turned cool and she was glad to have the warmth of a sweater as she drove through River Heights toward Riverside Park.

Usually the park was a popular recreation spot, but after parking her car outside the Park Drive

146

entrance, she saw that the cool, overcast weather had left the area deserted.

Glancing at her watch, Nancy said to herself, "Well, I'm on time. Now where is Jack Vernon?"

She walked slowly down the graveled path well into the park without seeing anyone on any of the park benches. There seemed to be no one within sight or sound. It was growing darker as Nancy turned and headed back toward the park entrance.

"*Oh!*" Suddenly she stopped short with a horrified gasp. Her sharp eyes had just glimpsed a sprawled form behind one of the benches, almost hidden by the shrubbery.

She ran quickly to the unconscious man and, taking a flashlight from her purse, shone it on his face. *It was Jack Vernon, badly bruised!*

# 15

## Three-Way Meeting

Nancy gasped in horror. She tried to revive the unconscious man, but soon gave up—he had been too badly hurt.

Her pulse racing anxiously, Nancy stood up. She remembered passing a booth on Park Drive just before reaching the park entrance. Nancy ran there and dialed the police.

"Don't worry about calling for an ambulance, Miss, we'll send one," the desk sergeant responded. "Just give me the location."

Nancy thought of Kim Vernon and took time to phone her. Kim was badly shaken by the news, but was grateful for the call. After arranging to meet her at the hospital, Nancy ran back to where Jack Vernon lay injured.

Within minutes, she heard the wail of sirens and saw the flashing lights of a police patrol car. Then an ambulance pulled up behind it. Police Chief McGinnis also arrived.

"Oh, Chief, I'm so glad you're here!" Nancy exclaimed. "I was going to call you!"

"The desk sergeant alerted me as soon as he realized who the victim was," McGinnis replied. "Politicians are public figures, and a case like this can really give River Heights a bad name!"

The young sleuth quickly filled him in. "Mr. Vernon and I were going to discuss the case I'm working on, so he suggested we meet here for privacy. I suspect someone wanted to stop him from telling me something."

"This was no ordinary mugging, then?"

Nancy shook her head. "I don't think so. Otherwise, why would the attacker have bothered to shove his victim out of sight? I believe whoever did it knew I was coming and hoped I wouldn't notice Mr. Vernon lying behind the bench. I almost didn't!"

It was Chief McGinnis's turn to frown. "If the attacker knew about your meeting, that raises the question of how he found out. Where and how did you make the appointment?"

"In person, at his campaign office."

149

"Hmm. Sounds like someone eaves-dropped—or his office might be bugged." Chief McGinnis said he would call the Bradley police and have them make an electronic sweep of the premises.

The teenage sleuth drove to Riverside Hospital. There she found a frightened Kim waiting anxiously for word on her brother's condition. Presently the emergency room doctor said he was in no danger. "But he'll have to stay here for further tests and observation."

Since Jack had been sedated, Nancy gave up any hope of questioning him that evening. She left Kim sitting by his bedside and went home.

The next morning Chief McGinnis called to report that the Bradley police had discovered an electronic listening device in his desk lamp.

"There's no evidence his political opponent had the place bugged," McGinnis said, "but we'll investigate that angle. Incidentally, we've had no luck so far, Nancy, in tracing that squint-eyed hood who attacked your housekeeper."

This reminded Nancy of the intruder who had invaded Eugene Horvath's island estate on Tuesday night. She told McGinnis about the incident and said, "If Mr. Horvath's right, that crook's name could be Sweeney Flint. Does that ring any bells?"

"Hmm." Chief McGinnis was silent for a while.

"I'm not sure, but it does sound vaguely familiar. Let me check it out and get back to you."

"Thank you, Chief. I'd appreciate that."

Nancy was just finishing her breakfast when Bess Marvin dropped in. The plump blond girl was all agog for details of her friend's exciting if unpleasant adventure the night before.

Nancy was surprised. "How did you hear about it?"

"On the morning newscast. After all, you're Nancy Drew, the famous girl detective, and Jack Vernon's running for state office—that's the stuff headlines are made of!"

"Oh, Bess." Nancy chuckled. "Come and have a cup of coffee and I'll tell you all about it."

Minutes later, the phone rang. When Nancy answered it, she got another surprise. The caller was Brett Hulme. He sounded tense.

"You're right, Nancy. It's time to talk. A bomb was planted in my car last night. It went off as I opened the door to get in. Luckily it was a dud, or else the wiring was bad. Anyhow, the damage was only slight."

"Thank goodness for that," Nancy breathed. "Brett, if you're ready to talk, I think someone else should be in on our discussion—Kim Vernon. Would you agree to all three of us meeting?"

"Of course . . . if she wants to see me."

"I'm sure she will!" Instantly Nancy hung up and dialed Kim, hoping to catch her at home. The golf star answered and eagerly agreed to a meeting that very morning.

When all was arranged, Nancy turned to Bess. "Whew! You heard all that? I think we're really going to get somewhere now."

"Let me know how everything comes out, Nancy. And by the way, can you drop me off at home on your way to Kim's?"

"Of course."

Just as the two girls were starting out the door, the busy telephone pealed again. Tad Farr was on the line, sounding upbeat and excited. "Good news, Nancy! Mom's made a full recovery!"

"Oh wonderful, Tad! She can talk now?"

"You bet! And she's anxious to talk to *you*. Any chance you could make it over to New York?"

"What about later this afternoon?"

"Great, I was hoping you'd say that!"

"I'll be there," Nancy promised. Hanging up, she told Bess, who was more eager than ever to be kept informed of the progress of the case.

"I'll keep you posted." Nancy grinned as she stopped her car in front of the Marvins' house.

"Call me before you leave New York, okay?" Bess asked.

Nancy agreed and was soon on her way to Kim's riverside cottage.

Kim was alone when Nancy arrived. Her cheeks were slightly flushed, from nervousness. In her rose pink T-shirt and faded jeans, with her dark hair curling about her face, she looked to Nancy more like a shy, pretty high-school girl of her own age than a famous golfer.

Brett Hulme rang the bell moments later, and Kim went to answer the door. From their words and manner, it was apparent to Nancy that both were deeply moved and happy to be seeing each other again, despite the unpleasant circumstances that had brought them together. The young detective felt surer than ever that they were still in love.

"Suppose you begin first, Kim," said Nancy as they settled themselves to talk—Nancy in a chintz-covered armchair, Brett and Kim on the sofa. "Tell us whatever you know that may have led up to last night's attack on your brother."

Kim's voice trembled slightly as she told how she and Jack had lost their parents in an accident soon after she turned pro. With her golf winnings, which were still meager at that time, she had helped to put him through graduate school, where he was majoring in political science. But their financial situation was precarious, and Jack felt guilty about living off his sister's generosity. "That's really what led up to all the trouble."

"By 'trouble,' do you mean the theft of Madame Arachne's jeweled spider?" Nancy asked gently.

Kim was startled that Nancy knew about the theft, but merely nodded, her expression tense and unhappy. "Yes. You see, *my brother was the one who stole it!* I was playing in a tournament near Oceanview when it happened. Jack came to me late that night and told me the whole story."

Kim related that he had been attending the festival with his university glee club. He told her he had been approached by a man who claimed to be a publicity agent working for Madame Arachne. The opera star's career was fading, it seemed, and she was no longer receiving the acclaim she craved and felt was her proper due.

"The publicity man told Jack he was secretly arranging a fake jewel robbery to put her back in the headlines. The plan called for Madame Arachne to stage a loud emotional scene when she discovered that her jeweled spider was gone. The police and TV news reporters would then be alerted immediately. But the brooch would be 'found' soon afterward as if the thief had accidentally dropped it."

"Wait!" put in Nancy. "Are you saying this so-called publicity man wanted your brother to commit the robbery?"

"Exactly—but only as a hoax. He said everything would be arranged to make it easy. The door of Madame Arachne's dressing room would be left open, and so on. And if Jack would carry out the plan, he would be paid a lot."

Kim stifled a sob. "It was terribly foolish! Jack should never have agreed to the scheme. And he soon regretted it! But he was struggling to finish his studies, and this seemed like an easy way to earn some money."

His first shock, Kim went on to explain, came as he was lifting the brooch from a jewel box on Madame Arachne's dressing table. An electronic flash went off, and Jack realized that his photo must have been snapped by a hidden burglar alarm device. This probably meant an alarm signal had been buzzed to the theater's security office or the Oceanview police station, so he didn't take time to find and destroy the photo. In his panicky state, he felt he had to get away fast.

Although he had managed to leave without being noticed, and had handed over the brooch to the fake publicity man lurking outside in the darkness behind the stage shell, another shock was in store. The police were called, and television news crews soon arrived, but the jeweled spider was never found as had been promised.

"By now," Kim said, "Jack was beginning to realize he'd been tricked into pulling a big-time theft. But no one came to arrest him, so he assumed his face hadn't been recognized from the alarm photo. That's why he came to see me—to ask my advice about what he should do."

"What did you tell him?" Nancy asked.

Kim said she had gone the next day to see Madame Arachne in Oceanview and made a clean breast of her brother's unintentional crime. She promised to pay back the cost of the jeweled spider out of her golf winnings, if only Madame Arachne would not turn Jack over to the police.

Much to her relief, the prima donna had merely smiled and patted her shoulder, saying, "Never mind, dear. Your brother was a victim too. Luckily my brooch was insured, so let the insurance company worry about paying me back and we'll say no more about it!"

But Kim's relief had been short-lived. A letter was waiting in her mail slot when she got back to her motel. It contained a print of the alarm photo, showing her brother's look of dismay as the camera snapped him redhanded in the act of filching the jeweled spider.

"So far," Kim added, "the thief in the picture apparently hadn't been recognized as a member of the university glee club. But to me the letter meant just one thing. The fake publicity agent hadn't only trapped Jack into committing a real robbery—somehow he'd gotten a copy of the alarm photo. So now he had evidence that could convict my brother and send him to prison!"

Confirming her fears was an enclosed message saying: SOMEDAY I'LL GIVE YOU AN ORDER—JUST OBEY IT AND NOTHING WILL HAPPEN TO YOUR BROTHER!

During the three years since then, while she was perfecting her golf game and gradually rising to top rank among women golf pros, Kim said she had received several nastily playful reminders of her brother's theft of the jeweled spider.

Nancy said quietly, "Including a drawing of a spider, and a live red spider in a plastic box?"

Kim's eyes widened momentarily. "Russ told you about those incidents, did he?"

"Yes. What I still don't know is why you dropped out of the Charleston match."

Kim drew a deep, unhappy sigh, her fingers kneading her tea napkin. "Halfway through the tournament, I got another blackmail message ordering me *not* to win."

"Any idea why?" asked Nancy.

"It's not hard to guess. By that time I was well in the lead. I'm sure the blackmailer must have placed a big gambling bet at heavy odds—*against* my winning!"

Kim had been too proud and honest to throw the match deliberately. Yet she didn't dare risk ruining her brother's political career—and perhaps wrecking his expected marriage to Senator Hawthorn's daughter—by defying the blackmailer. "So I felt the only way out was for me to withdraw from the tournament," Kim said.

Nancy pondered thoughtfully for a moment, then said, "Let's assume you're right, that the fake publicity agent who trapped your brother is also the blackmailer. Any idea who he might be?"

Kim gave a helpless shrug. "All I know is the name he told Jack when he first approached him —Sweeney Flint."

# 16

## Maggie's Secret

*Sweeney Flint!* So the fake publicity man was the same person who had tried to attack Madame Arachne's husband—and was very likely also the squint-eyed thief Nancy had caught tampering with Kim's golf bag!

Another thought struck the girl sleuth. Maybe the object which the thief had dropped in the grass had been a red toy spider!

If her guess was right, he must have intended to slip it in the pocket of the golf bag as a warning to Kim not to talk. And the cobwebbed racket had been an even stronger warning!

Wrenching her thoughts back to the present, Nancy looked at Brett Hulme. "So much for

Kim's story. Would you like to tell us now what-ever you know that might help?"

Brett nodded. "First of all, Nancy, you're right. I did design that jeweled spider brooch for Madame Arachne. She wanted it to be as realistic as possible, and she also wanted it to be a ruby spider, since that was her birthstone." He chuck-led wryly. "So I researched various kinds of red spiders, but I still wound up mostly using my imagination!"

However, Brett continued, he knew nothing about Jack Vernon's part in the theft of the brooch until recently, when Simon Shand walked into his shop one day and commissioned him to design a silver cobweb necklace.

"He said he wanted it made so that Madame Arachne's ruby spider would fit on it, as if the two had been designed to go together. I asked him what was the point, since the jeweled spider had been stolen three years ago."

"And what did Mr. Shand say?" Nancy asked.

"He just chuckled nastily and said, 'That's what the public thinks, but I happen to know that so-called robbery was just a scam! The whole thing was cooked up by a slick con artist named Sweeney Flint.' He said Madame Arachne had needed money at the time, so she sold the jeweled

spider to a wealthy collector named Oscar Larue—"

"She *sold* the jeweled spider?" Nancy broke in.

"So Shand said. And also that she had a fake
robbery staged in case any reporter or photo-
grapher started asking embarrassing questions
about what had happened to her beautiful ruby
spider brooch. He also mentioned that Flint had
tricked a fellow named Jack Vernon into pulling
the robbery, and that Jack was the famous golf
star's brother and was now running for State As-
sembly. Shand talked as if it was a joke!"

"But how did he learn all that?" asked Kim
with a shocked expression.

"From the wealthy collector, Oscar Larue. He
said Larue had recently suffered a fatal illness,
but before he passed away, he'd agreed to sell the
jeweled spider to Shand—provided he would
promise not to let any word about the phony
robbery leak out. In fact that's partly why Shand
was having me make the silver cobweb necklace."

Nancy frowned. "I'm not sure I follow you."

"To keep the jeweled spider from being recognized, I mean. You see, Shand's engaged to a
Broadway showgirl. He wanted to give her the
ruby spider as an engagement gift, and he figured no one would recognize it as Madame

Arachne's brooch if it was mounted on a silver cobweb necklace."

"But wouldn't he be taking a chance?" queried Nancy. "What if someone *did* recognize it?"

Brett Hulme shrugged. "That didn't worry Shand. He claims he has a written bill of sale to cover its purchase from Oscar Larue, and that Larue, in turn, had a written bill of sale to prove *he* bought the spider from Madame Arachne."

Brett went on, "Needless to say, I hadn't much taste for designing the cobweb necklace under those circumstances. But I agreed to do so, if only to keep any other jewelry designer from learning how the spider came into Shand's possession. However, after that rock was thrown through my window, I got a mysterious phone call."

"From whom?" said Nancy.

"I don't know," Brett puzzled. "It made no sense at first. The caller demanded to know what happened to the jeweled spider. He warned me I'd better tell the truth, or I'd get something a lot worse than a rock aimed at my head—and next time he wouldn't miss!"

"So what did you say?"

"I told him Simon Shand had the brooch. Then he snarled, 'Don't give me that! All Shand has is a cheap glass imitation!' Well, I kept telling

163

him I knew nothing more about it. I guess I finally convinced him. Anyhow, he hung up."

Nancy mused, "Could the car bombing have been a follow-up to his phone threat?"

"I doubt it." Brett explained that last night's bomb blast had been followed by another menacing phone call—but this time the voice was entirely different. "And he said his name was *Sweeney Flint!*"

Nancy's eyes widened with excitement. The mysterious con man's name seemed to be cropping up in all sorts of connections! "What did he have to say?" she asked.

"Apparently he's also looking for the jeweled spider. And he too knew that the one Simon Shand has is just a glass fake."

"But why was he calling *you?*" Nancy persisted.

"Because he figured Jack Vernon and I were the only other two people besides himself who knew anything about the phony theft. Therefore, it must have been one of us who'd arranged to switch a fake spider for the real one. But I kept telling him I knew nothing about it, just as I'd told the first caller, so finally he hung up."

Nancy mulled over what Brett Hulme had just told her. With these latest frightening developments, it seemed as though the puzzle was becoming more complicated than ever!

"What about Simon Shand himself?" she said, looking up at Brett. "Did he sound as if he knew about the glass counterfeit when he phoned you to cancel the order for the silver cobweb?"

"Definitely! That's why he canceled the order," Brett replied. "He was pretty sore about getting stuck with a fake. But he also seemed convinced that the spider Oscar Larue sold him was genuine—in other words, that someone had stolen it from him later on and substituted a glass imitation."

"Did he notify the police?"

Again Brett grinned wryly. "No way! His business crowd's a pretty tough bunch, I guess, and he didn't want them to find out how he'd been cheated. He was afraid that if the news leaked out, it might make him look like an easy mark. It would also be embarrassing to him."

Nancy was silent for several moments. Then she mused aloud, "The mystery seems to boil down to two main questions. One: how and when did the glass fake get substituted for the real jeweled spider? If it happened early on, was the brooch Oscar Larue bought from Madame Arachne the real one—or a glass counterfeit?"

"Since both of them are dead now, how can we ever hope to find out?" Kim murmured.

"That remains to be seen," said Nancy. "But

the other question's just as important, or maybe more so."

"What's that?"

"Who has the real jeweled spider now? We're going to have to find the answers to both questions, Kim, if we hope to clear your brother!"

Nancy drove away from the riverside cottage turning the questions over and over in her mind. After she had parked her car in the train station lot and bought her ticket to New York, she found she had a forty-minute wait until the train was due. Nancy used the time to get a sandwich and milkshake at a nearby luncheonette and arrived back just before the train pulled in.

On arriving in Manhattan, she took a taxi to the hospital. A smiling Tad Farr opened the door of his mother's room when she knocked.

"Hi, Nancy! Come on in!" As Maggie Farr, weak but smiling, held out a hand to their visitor, he went on, "We both want to thank you, Nancy. I'm sure the way you tried to help Mom communicate speeded her recovery."

Mrs. Farr nodded and squeezed Nancy's hand. "Tad's right. I'm grateful to you, my dear. You're a lovely girl."

"Thank you." Nancy blushed and smiled back. "But now we both want to hear your story."

Tad pulled up a chair for the teenage sleuth, and they both sat down at Maggie Farr's bedside.

The elderly woman explained that she had been present in Madame Arachne's hotel suite in Oceanview on the day Kim Vernon came to plead with the opera star on her brother's behalf.

Nancy was startled. "Then you know about him stealing her jeweled spider?"

"Indeed I do. Only that's *not* what he stole!"

Tad shot a puzzled glance at Nancy, who had a sudden flash of intuition. "What do you mean, Mom?" Tad started to ask.

But Nancy broke in, "I believe I can guess. What Jack Vernon stole was just a cheap glass imitation. Am I right, Mrs. Farr?"

"You bet you are!" Maggie responded. "That woman, Madame Arachne, was the most extravagant creature you ever saw! She spent money like there was no tomorrow. Cars, clothes, jewelry, gifts for her friends—anything that caught her eye, she'd buy. Money slipped through her fingers like water, so half the time she was flat broke. One day generous, next day mean and stingy as old Scrooge himself! Anyhow, one of those times when Madame O was broke, she sold off her ruby spider to some rich fella named Oscar Larue. That's why she had the

167

glass imitation made—so no one would know she'd had to raise money by selling her brooch!"

Nancy was shocked. "Then she deliberately misled Kim Vernon! I mean, she wouldn't even relieve Kim's mind by letting her know the brooch Jack took was just a fake of no value?"

"That's right, dear. Believe me, that was Madame Arachne all over. Here was her chance to put on a big act—as if she was a generous, kind-hearted, forgiving fairy godmother—so she played it to the hilt. If she'd told the truth, that would have meant admitting she'd pawned her real brooch for cash to stave off the bill collectors. Madame O would have eaten toads first!"

Once again, Nancy realized what a strange and complex, maddening yet fascinating person Madame Arachne Onides must have been. "Yet I suspect you liked her in spite of everything . . . didn't you, Mrs. Farr?"

Maggie smiled reminiscently. "Maybe so. She was always good to me, I'll say that for her—provided I put up with her tantrums. But the way she let Miss Vernon go on thinking her brother had stolen a priceless piece of jewelry—that disgusted me! When I saw that poor troubled girl's face on TV, I couldn't help wondering if the past had anything to do with her dropping out of the tournament. I guess it was a crazy idea, eh?"

"It certainly wasn't!" Nancy declared. "You've helped Kim Vernon so by telling me this, Mrs. Farr. She'll be very grateful!"

Before leaving, Nancy chatted a while longer with Tad and Maggie. Among other things, she learned that Renzo Scaglia had fallen deeply in love with the tempestuous prima donna. When Eugene Horvath became Arachne's business manager, however, and eventually talked her into marrying him, Scaglia had suffered a cruel disappointment.

Nancy remembered to call her chum from New York before starting home. "My flight will get in an hour from now, Bess. So let's have dinner, all right?"

"Super, Nancy! I'm going downtown with Mom later, so I can meet you anywhere."

"Then how about the front of Taylor's Department Store at six o'clock?"

"I'll be there!"

When the girls finally met, Bess observed Nancy's happy expression. "You look like the cat that swallowed the canary! Good news, huh?"

"Very good!" Nancy beamed. "I'll tell you all about it over dinner."

"Hey, that reminds me," Bess went on. "Chief

McGinnis called right after you did. He was trying to get in touch with you. He asked me to tell
you that Jack Vernon is well enough now to be
questioned."

"Oh great! Bess, I think I should drop over to
the hospital right away. Want to come along?"

Bess was more than willing, since this would
save time. The two girls hurried to Nancy's blue
car and headed for Riverside Hospital.

Moments later, as she glanced in the rearview
mirror, Nancy's heart gave a lurch.

Dangling close to her right ear by a silken
thread from the car ceiling, hung a fearsome,
deadly-looking spider!

# 17

## A Voice in the Dark

Nancy stifled the little cry of surprise and fear that rose in her throat. Her first impulse was to swing her shoulder bag upward to brush the frightful creature away from her, but then it might land on her or even Bess!

"Don't move or make a sound," Nancy advised her companion in a low, controlled voice.

"Hmm . . . what's the matt—" Bess replied, breaking off in a shriek as she turned her head from the side window and saw the horrid spider.

"Just stay calm, and reach in the glove compartment, will you?" Nancy said, sounding less nervous than she felt. "There's a paper bag in there, I think, with flashlight batteries in it."

Bess extracted the bag. "Is this what you mean?"

"Yes. Empty out the batteries, please, and hand me the empty bag." By now, Nancy had stopped the car and was opening her door. "I also suggest that you get out of the car for a second."

"Oh, Nancy, do be careful," Bess pleaded as she followed Nancy's instructions obediently. "Maybe we ought to call someone to help u—"

But her friend had already opened the paper bag, positioned it under the spider, and brought it swiftly upward so as to capture the creature inside it. Then she twisted the top and, after fishing in her purse, found a rubber band with which to hold the bag tightly closed.

Bess let out a long weakened gasp. "I could never have done that!"

Nancy burst into a merry peal of laughter. "Don't tell anyone, but I was scared, too!"

"Where on earth did it come from, Nancy?"

"Good question. It certainly didn't look like any plain old American variety. Maybe that spider expert, Paul Taggart, can tell us."

Because the famous girl detective had been the one who found Jack Vernon, she was readily permitted to see him. When Nancy phoned his room, he not only sounded eager to talk but told her she could bring Bess up as well, if she liked.

"I'm through hiding the past," the young politician declared when the two girls were seated at his bedside. "What happened last night has convinced me I should have made a clean breast to the police right from the first, instead of dumping the whole problem on Kim's shoulders."

"She's told me the whole story," Nancy said.

Jack Vernon nodded. "I know. And now I'm prepared to tell *my* story, even if it costs me the election . . . and my chance to marry Celia Hawthorn," he ended unhappily but firmly.

"I'm sure your fiancée will stand by you. But if you don't mind my offering a word of advice," Nancy counseled sympathetically, "I suggest you hold off a while longer before making any statement to the news media. I'm hoping my investigation of this case will clear your name completely."

"If you can do that, I'll be eternally grateful," the young candidate muttered in a husky voice.

Vernon related that after his recent political rally had been broken up by hecklers, he received a highly unpleasant phone call. "Whoever it was wanted to know what had happened to the *real* jeweled spider. He said the heckling was just a sample. If I didn't come clean, as he put it, he'd wreck my election campaign!"

"In other words," Nancy queried, "he knew all

about your part in the theft of the brooch from Madame Arachne's dressing room?"

"Right. So I told him I hadn't seen the brooch since I turned it over to that fake publicity agent, Sweeney Flint."

"Can you remember what Flint looked like?"

"How can I ever forget!" Jack said grimly, clenching his fist at the recollection. "His nose was sort of twisted, as if it had been broken and hadn't been set properly, and one eyelid drooped. He looked so sinister, I remember thinking he must have a tough time attracting publicity clients!"

This seemed to remove any doubt, Nancy reflected, that the mysterious Sweeney Flint was also the midnight intruder on Eugene Horvath's island estate.

"How did your phone caller react to what you told him?" she said aloud.

Jack Vernon shrugged. "I guess he believed me. Anyhow, he muttered a couple more threats about wrecking my campaign if I was lying, and hung up."

"Do you think he was responsible for last night's attack in the park?"

Jack frowned thoughtfully. "I doubt it."

"Why?"

"For one thing, the attacker asked me the same question the phone caller did." Vernon explained that while he was waiting for Nancy just inside the park entrance, he suddenly felt a knife at his back. "Then a voice behind me asked what had happened to the real jeweled spider. When I told him I hadn't seen it since the night of the theft, he told me he was going to teach me not to talk to snoops like you. Next thing I knew, something hit me hard on the back of the head! That's the last I remember till I came to in the hospital."

"You said 'for *one* thing,'" Nancy pursued. "Is there some other reason why you think he and your phone caller were different persons?"

"Yes—my assailant's voice," Jack said grimly. "It sounded vaguely familiar, but I couldn't place it. Now I've got a strong hunch who he was."

"Who do you think?" asked Nancy.

"Sweeney Flint!"

Bess Marvin had listened to Jack Vernon's story with breathless interest. Later, as she and her girlfriend were driving from the hospital to Paul Taggart's wooded estate, she murmured anxiously, "Do you think the same person who hurt Mr. Vernon could have put that spider in your car?"

"It's certainly possible, Bess. If the spider turns

176

out to be a foreign specimen, that'll convince me it didn't creep in all by itself!"

Nancy's suspicion turned out to be well founded.

"This is a wolf spider," Taggart announced after shaking it out of the paper bag. "And I can tell you just where it came from, Nancy."

"Where?"

"My collection. Someone broke in and took it last night. This spider happens to be quite harmless. Unfortunately, the other live specimen that was taken *isn't* quite so harmless."

"You mean two spiders were stolen?" the pretty young sleuth exclaimed in surprise.

"Yes." Taggart shot her a thoughtful glance. "The other one that's missing is a poisonous black widow!"

# 18

## Legal Evidence

Nancy felt shaken as she and Bess drove away from the arachnologist's sprawling stone house.

"Do you suppose whoever put that wolf spider in your car *knew* it was harmless?" asked Bess.

"Just what I was wondering," Nancy confessed. "Let's be thankful it wasn't the black widow!"

"How do we know he didn't put *that* in your car, too?" Bess blurted in a quavering voice.

As the two girls exchanged startled looks, Nancy jammed her foot on the brake pedal. Then she hastily pulled over to the side of the road. "We'd better make sure right now!"

After a careful search, Nancy felt satisfied that the poisonous creature was not lurking in her beloved blue sports car. She and Bess breathed sighs of relief. Nevertheless, the scary experience somewhat spoiled their planned evening of fun.

When Nancy returned home, she found her father reading in his usual chair. She asked if he had ever heard of Oscar Larue.

"Yes, he was well known in the business world up until a few years ago," said Carson Drew. "Then he retired and spent his time collecting antique cars. I believed he was rumored to have lost a lot of money in the stock market before he died. Why?"

Nancy related what Simon Shand had told Brett Hulme about how Larue had bought Madame Arachne's jeweled spider and later sold it to Shand. "Is there any way to check out his story, Dad?"

"Hmm." Mr. Drew frowned thoughtfully. "If I can learn the name of the attorney who handled Larue's estate and explain to him that you're working on a mystery case, he might be willing to answer a few questions. Let me see what I can find out."

"Thanks, Dad. If you can, it'll be a big help!"

Nancy was still turning the day's events over in her mind as she drifted off to sleep. Both Jack Vernon and Brett Hulme had been threatened and attacked by two separate, unknown enemies.

179

In Jack's case, that second enemy might have been the mysterious Sweeney Flint. Was he also responsible for the bomb planted in Brett's car?

If so, maybe the first mystery caller had also been the same in both cases. Nancy was beginning to suspect who that person might be.

Next morning, as soon as she finished breakfast, she dialed Simon Shand's number, intending to ask for an appointment. His servant answered, however, and told her his employer had gone to Oceanview for the last few days of the festival.

I may just have to chase down there after him, Nancy decided crossly. Then she brightened. Why don't I ask Bess and George to come with me and see the opera Saturday night?

The teenage sleuth was just pouring herself another glass of juice when the phone rang. Carson Drew was calling from his office.

"The executor of Oscar Larue's estate is an attorney named Howard Emmett," Mr. Drew reported. "He practices in New York and most of his court cases are heard there, but he also has a suburban law office in Mapleton, since a good many of his clients reside in this state. I've already spoken to him, Nancy, and he's agreed to

180

see you at his Mapleton office at ten forty-five. Can you make it?"

"You bet, Dad—and thanks ever so much!"

Howard Emmett proved to be a stout, balding man with shrewd gray eyes and pinch-nose glasses. He greeted Nancy with a friendly smile, invited her to have a chair, and asked how he could be of help.

"Dad's probably told you about the mystery case I'm working on, counsellor. According to an informant, Oscar Larue bought a valuable ruby brooch in the shape of a spider from the opera singer, Madame Arachne Onides. Can you confirm that story?"

"Yes," Emmett nodded. "Among his effects was a bill of sale for such a brooch from Madame Onides for a price of three hundred thousand dollars."

"I see." Nancy hesitated. "Are you aware that that brooch was later reported to have been stolen from her while she was performing at the Oceanview Festival?"

Emmett's face took on a troubled frown. "Yes, indeed I am. It would be inappropriate, however, for me to comment on exactly what may or may not have been taken at that time."

Nancy realized that his discretion as a lawyer would prevent him from charging Madame Arachne with a hoax or outright fraud, even if she had lied in claiming that the stolen object had been her original jeweled spider. "I'm also informed," she went on, "that your late client, Mr. Larue, sold the brooch just before he died to Simon Shand."

"Yes, that too is correct," said Attorney Emmett. "In fact, the cashier's check from Mr. Shand was still in my client's possession and had not yet been deposited in the bank when he suffered his fatal heart attack."

"Then how do you account for the fact that the brooch which Mr. Shand now has is only a cheap glass counterfeit?"

"*What!*" Attorney Emmett was clearly shocked by Nancy's question. "Are you sure of that?"

The young detective nodded. "The person who told me so had it from Mr. Shand himself."

Howard Emmett frowned again and drummed his fingers on the desk. "All I can say is that I'm quite sure the brooch my client sold Mr. Shand was the same one he bought from Madame Onides."

"Is there any chance *that* might have been a fake?"

"Highly unlikely! Whenever Mr. Larue was about to purchase any jewelry, he was always careful to have it examined first by an expert appraiser. He was too shrewd to be tricked or cheated."

"In other words, if a switch was made, it must have been *after* Mr. Shand bought the brooch?"

"Correct!"

Nancy was silent a moment. Then, on a sudden impulse, she said, "Was there anything among Mr. Larue's papers indicating he might have known someone named Sweeney Flint?"

"Hmm." Emmett reflected. "That name is not known to me. One way to find out, of course, might be to check the names and phone numbers in my client's desk book."

"Could I look through it?" Nancy asked eagerly.

Emmett said the desk book and all of Larue's private papers were now being stored in a New York bank vault while his estate was being probated. But he promised to arrange with the bank for her to see the book on Monday.

Nancy thanked the lawyer and left his office. That afternoon she called her two girlfriends and invited them to go with her to Oceanview on Saturday. Bess had to beg off since an uncle was arriving to visit her family over the weekend. But George jumped at the idea.

Luckily the two girls were able to make overnight reservations at the same motel where they had stayed before. A call to Renzo Scaglia also helped them obtain tickets to the opera.

They set out from River Heights late on Saturday morning and arrived in Oceanview in time to enjoy lunch in a restaurant overlooking the harbor. Then Nancy prepared to look up Simon Shand.

"Do you know where to find him?" George asked.

"His servant said he was staying at the Beachfront Plaza Hotel." Much to Nancy's annoyance, however, there was no answer when she called his room on the house phone, and the desk clerk reported seeing him go out just before lunch.

Nancy kept calling throughout the afternoon, but with no luck. "Maybe we can spot him at the opera tonight," her chum suggested.

The girls were enthralled by the opening scenes of *Carmen*. In the crowded lobby during the intermission, Nancy suddenly touched George's arm and whispered, "There he is!"

Simon Shand was at the counter, buying refreshments for himself and his showgirl fiancée.

"Well, well, well! If it isn't little Miss Sherlock!" he said on seeing Nancy.

"Could we talk for a moment?" she asked.

"Sure thing. Got news to report?"

Nancy felt being subtle with the trucking tycoon would be a waste of time. Instead, she hoped to startle the truth out of him. So she bluntly asked if he was responsible for the rock thrown at Brett Hulme, or the heckling that had broken up Jack Vernon's campaign rally.

Shand chuckled cynically. "I knew you were smart, girlie! I'd deny it in court, mind you, but just between the two of us, sure, I hired strong-arm men to pull both jobs."

Since Nancy knew about his purchase of the jeweled spider, Shand no longer seemed to feel any need to be secretive about the brooch. He admitted trying to frighten the young jewelry designer and politician in order to find out if either had had anything to do with stealing the real brooch from him and substituting the fake. But he denied having anything to do with Jack Vernon's beating or the bomb planted in Brett's car.

"At first I figured Kim Vernon might have hired Sweeney Flint to get back the brooch, so she could clear her brother. I thought he might have been going to slip it in her golf bag when you spotted him at the country club," Shand told Nancy. "But now I doubt if she knows any more than her brother or Brett Hulme does."

"Are you saying you *recognized* Sweeney Flint that day at the country club?" Nancy asked keenly.

"I've never met him in person, but I've heard what he looks like," Shand replied. "He's one of the slickest crooks in this part of the country. If you can nail him and get back my jeweled spider, I'll pay you a ten grand reward!"

In her motel room that night, Nancy mulled over the mystery. Shand still seemed to think Sweeney Flint had succeeded in getting his hands on the real ruby brooch. Yet if her own theory was right that Flint was behind the second attacks on Jack Vernon and Brett Hulme, this meant he too was hunting for the real jeweled spider.

Nancy soon fell asleep. She awakened with a start, feeling something on her arm. She was about to brush it away when a frightening thought struck her. Nancy switched on the bed-side lamp—then gasped with fear.

An eight-legged creature was crawling up her arm. *It was a poisonous black widow spider!*

# *19*

## *The Face at the Window*

Nancy struggled to control her fright and disgust. She realized she must keep calm. "George!" she gasped, and then when her friend didn't wake, she called, "George!" again more loudly.

"Wha . . . What?" George sat upright in bed, rubbing her eyes.

"Help me!" Nancy said, keeping her eyes on the terrifying creature. By now, it had almost reached her shoulder!

George started to ask what was wrong—then gasped in dismay as she saw the spider.

"It's a black widow!" Nancy said. "Get the bathroom glass and turn on all the lights!"

Swiftly, George did as her friend asked. Then Nancy flicked the spider from her arm onto the white sheet, and George quickly imprisoned it under the inverted glass!

"Whew!" Nancy breathed a sigh of relief, then jumped out of bed and ran to the bathroom to get the waxed paper bag that had been used to seal the clean glass.

With this as a cover, held tightly in place by a rubber band, the spider was soon safely bottled up and consigned to the medicine cabinet overnight.

"Bess told me about the spider in your car," George said, still wide-eyed. "This must be the other one that was stolen, right?"

Nancy nodded. "Whoever did it obviously slipped the black widow into our room while we were at the opera."

The next morning as they drove back to River Heights, George insisted on holding the glass. "I'll feel safer being able to see where this little black devil is!" she said ruefully.

Paul Taggart was both grateful and apologetic when they returned the poisonous creature to his collection. "From now on, I'll redouble security—especially on *this* specimen!" he promised.

On Monday morning, Nancy prepared for her trip to the New York bank to examine Oscar

Larue's desk book. In case this might lead to a further investigation in Manhattan or its surrounding area, she packed a small overnight bag and promised Hannah she would call her from the city. After breakfast she set out with her father, who was to drop her off at the train station on the way to his law office.

"Nancy dear, be careful. And call me if you need anything," Carson Drew said as he kissed his daughter good-bye.

At the bank and trust company in New York, Nancy was referred to Mr. Corder, a dignified, taciturn bank officer, who took her to a room downstairs and seated her at a table. Then he disappeared, presumably to enter the vault and get the book which Attorney Howard Emmett had arranged for her to see. He soon came back, handed her the item in question, and sat down in an armchair in one corner of the room, where he busied himself in studying a sheaf of financial statements.

Nancy, meanwhile, began leafing through Oscar Larue's desk book. Her pulse skittered as she came to the F's, and a moment later, her tense expression burst into a grin of satisfaction. Among the names listed was that of Sweeney Flint!

No address was given, but there was a phone number opposite his name. After writing down the number, Nancy gave the book back to Mr. Corder and smilingly thanked him. He unbent enough to return her smile.

Before leaving the bank, Nancy went to a phone booth in the lobby and dialed Flint's number. A woman's nasal voice answered.

"Sweeney Flint? Nah. Never heard of him," she responded to Nancy's query. "Must be an old listing—I've had this number for the last six months." And the woman hung up curtly.

Nancy realized then that tracing the mysterious Sweeney Flint was not going to be quick and easy. She decided to find a hotel room.

Once located and settled in her room, Nancy called Hannah to let the housekeeper know where she was staying. Then she set about getting information from the telephone company. A few calls, however, soon convinced her that the company was extremely reticent when it came to giving out data on its subscribers.

Nancy sat with her chin in her hand and thought. "Looks like I'm going to need contacts on this case," she said to herself. "Maybe I should start with Police Chief McGinnis."

Her spirits rose as the chief answered her ring

cheerfully. "Matter of fact, I was going to call *you* this afternoon, Nancy. I have a good friend in the New York Police Department. Through him, I just found out that Sweeney Flint's a known con man. But he's never been caught, so they have no record on him—no arrests, no photo, no finger-prints!"

"Gee," Nancy said, "I have his old phone number, but the telephone company won't give me any address to go with it."

"Well, I'm sure my friend can help. Detective Al Barnwell, his name is. Give me the number and let me call him. Then either he or I'll get back to you."

While she waited, Nancy had lunch sent up to her room. She had just finished eating and was pacing the floor restlessly when the phone rang.

"Al Barnwell here, Miss Drew. Sorry to have taken so long, but I have the information. That phone was installed in the Mantell Building on East Twentieth." He gave her the exact address and added, "Not a very good neighborhood. The building's owned by Eisman & Luft. If I can help you any further, let me know."

After thanking him and promising to pass on any information she gleaned on Sweeney Flint, Nancy hung up.

At last she had something to work on! Snatching up her purse, she went down in the elevator, turned in her key at the desk, and hurried out to catch a taxi. By the time she paid off the cabby in front of the Mantell Building, it was 4:00 P.M. Nancy pushed open the door and went in.

The dim little lobby offered an elevator and a stairway. Rather than trust the creaky lift, she walked up to the next floor and opened the first door she came to with a business name on it.

A droopy-jowled man with lank hair looked up from some papers he was shuffling. Nancy asked if he remembered a tenant named Sweeney Flint.

"Nope, just been here a month myself. Better check with the landlord."

"How about the janitor or superintendent?"

"You kidding? You can never find those bums! They wouldn't know, anyhow, so why waste your time? Check with the landlord, like I said." He gave her the address and resumed sorting papers

By now, the rush hour traffic was in full swing. Nancy battled through it but found it impossible to catch a cab, so she ended up walking the twenty-odd blocks to the building in which the firm of Eisman & Luft was located.

"Sorry, girlie—we're closing," a fat, cigar-chewing man told her as she walked in their offices. When Nancy asked about tracing a tenant, he laughed. "I doubt we have any record, but you can check back tomorrow. Leave your name, if you like."

Nancy made her way back to the hotel glumly.

"Nancy!" a familiar voice greeted her as she entered the lobby.

"Ned! Oh, Ned! How good to see you! Is anything wrong?"

Ned laughed. "Not a thing, now that you're here!" He gave her a big hug, then added, "Eugene Horvath's been trying to reach you. He's gotten some fresh threats and he's frightened. But he thinks that with your help, he may be able to trap the crook. So he asked me to find you."

"Will you come with me to the island, Ned?"

"You bet! His cruiser will pick us up at the Battery pier."

After a brief discussion, Nancy hastily got her things from her room and checked out of the hotel, while Ned rustled up some food for them to eat on the boat. Half an hour later, they were boarding Horvath's motor cruiser.

With his chauffeur-valet, Sandor, at the helm, the boat was soon plowing its way out of New York Harbor. Nancy and Ned enjoyed the gorgeous sunset as they ate.

Dusk had closed in and night was falling by the

193

time they reached Moonlight Island. They found Eugene Horvath waiting tensely in the den of his beautiful Greek-columned mansion.

He bounded to his feet as they entered, his face twitching with fear. "Thank heavens you're here!" he exclaimed. "The radio-telephone's gone dead, and a few minutes ago I saw Sweeney Flint's face at the window!"

# 20

## Island Peril

"That's impossible, sir—it must have been your imagination!" Sandor tried to calm his master. "There's nowhere else on the island a boat could land, except in the cove. And I assure you there was none in sight. Your guests will confirm that." Nancy and Ned both nodded.

"At all other points around the island, anyone who tried to land would find only sheer rock cliffs," Sandor added logically.

"Don't try to tell me what I saw or didn't see!" Horvath's voice cracked from nervous tension as his temper rose. "Last time he came by submarine."

"But I planted sonobuoys in the cove this morning, sir," Sandor stated patiently. "Any boat that enters is immediately detected by sonar and sets off an alarm in the house. Did you not hear the alarm buzzer when our cruiser arrived?"

"Yes, yes. No doubt your alarm system is very ingenious!" As Horvath paced back and forth, he snatched a cigar from a humidor on his desk. "Nevertheless, no system is foolproof. What if an intruder swam out to the island using scuba gear?"

The stony-faced chauffeur shrugged. "Whatever you say, Mr. Horvath. If you think an enemy's lurking outside, I'll go and look for him. Perhaps Mr. Nickerson will help me search?"

"Glad to," said Ned.

When they were gone, Eugene Horvath briefly resumed his frantic attempts to call for help.

"Ned told me you've received more threats, Mr. Horvath," put in Nancy.

"Yes—more phone calls from that maniac, Sweeney Flint!" Horvath had lit his cigar while Sandor went to get flashlights; it was clamped between his teeth now as he looked up at Nancy. "I received one call last evening, one around midnight, and another this morning. The scoundrel's obviously trying to frighten me."

"And you want my help in trapping him. What sort of plan do you have in mind?"

Horvath removed his cigar from his mouth and regarded its glowing tip for a moment. A cunning look came into his eyes. "First, tell me—has your sleuthing turned up any further clues?"

Nancy nodded. "Sweeney Flint was behind the theft of your wife's jeweled spider. Oddly enough," Nancy went on, "your wife had sold her ruby brooch to a millionaire collector named Oscar Larue *before* the robbery occurred."

There was a moment of startled silence. Then Horvath said, "In that case, what was stolen?"

"A cheap glass imitation. Her dresser, Maggie Farr, says she had a fake ruby spider made to keep people from finding out she'd been forced to sell the real brooch.

"I'm told Madame Arachne was very extravagant and spendthrift," Nancy explained. "She sold the brooch to raise cash at a time when she was broke and badly needed money."

Horvath's eyes narrowed. "Really?"

Nancy nodded again. "Among Mr. Larue's papers was a bill of sale from your wife. The strange thing is, he also had Sweeney Flint's name and phone number in his desk book.

"I happen to know Sweeney Flint master-minded the theft of the imitation brooch," Nancy added. "And the fact that Larue knew him suggests he was also involved in the sale of the *real* brooch. My guess is, Sweeney Flint acted as go-between when Madame Arachne sold her jeweled spider to Oscar Larue . . . and then talked her into staging a fake robbery so she could collect from the insurance company."

Horvath stared at the young detective through a wreath of cigar smoke. "My dear Miss Drew," he said, "you make it sound as though Sweeney Flint was a close friend and advisor of my wife!"

"*More* than a close friend and advisor." Nancy gazed at her host calmly. "I think she married him. In fact I'm now convinced 'Sweeney Flint' is just an alias of Eugene Horvath!"

There was a long moment of silence, broken at last by Horvath's low chuckle. "Well, well! Quite a sensational accusation. Can you prove it?"

"I'm sure I can," Nancy said coolly. "You see, Mr. Horvath, you made a slight mistake.

When I first mentioned her jeweled spider, you pretended to know nothing about it. Yet that color photo, which you look at every day, shows her ruby brooch in the shape of a spider very clearly!"

"Dear me, so it does!" Eugene Horvath chuckled unpleasantly. "Well, Miss Drew, I've realized for some time that you were becoming a nuisance. That's why I'm going to get rid of you!"

"Just one thing I don't understand," said Nancy. "Why have you gone on tormenting Kim Vernon?"

"Tormenting? What a nasty word, my dear! Miss Vernon's golfing prowess is highly valuable to me."

Horvath explained that when he had first tricked Jack Vernon into committing the phony theft, he suddenly realized he could use the evidence against Jack to blackmail his sister.

"It was already clear that Kim was heading for golf stardom," he went on. "But I waited patiently until she became the top U.S. woman golfer. Now, by controlling whether she wins or loses, I can fix the outcome of major tournaments—just as I did in the Charleston match—and clean up on bets!"

To keep Kim frightened enough to obey orders, Horvath would send her mocking reminders of the crime for which her brother could be sent to prison. "Actually, Sandor and I have been partners in crime for many years. Both of us, at

200

different times, have used a putty nose and taped-down eyelid to pose as Sweeney Flint."

It was Sandor in disguise, Horvath said, who had tried to plant a red plastic spider in Kim's golf bag as a warning not to talk too freely to reporters. Later he had delivered the cobwebbed tennis racket.

It was also the chauffeur who had planted the bomb in Brett's car and assaulted Jack Vernon in the park. The purpose was to confuse Nancy and convince her that "Sweeney Flint" really existed—but that he did not have the spider.

Horvath opened his desk drawer and took out the missing brooch. Nancy gasped in sheer awe and admiration at the beautifully crafted ornament. The spider's ruby body glowed with a fiery radiance. Its diamond-crusted legs sparkled like a myriad of ice crystals in a blaze of mountain sunlight.

"Breathtaking, isn't it?" Horvath murmured. "How could anyone who once saw such a lovely work of art ever forget it! Now you can understand how I felt when I heard that Simon Shand had bought the spider from Oscar Larue and was planning to let his fiancée wear it in public. The brooch was *bound* to be recognized. And once that news got back to the insurance company, an investigation was sure to follow. They'd have found out Arachne bilked them out of half a million dollars for the theft of a glass counterfeit. I'd have faced a choice between paying back the money or even going to prison myself as an accomplice in the fraud!"

Nancy nodded. "I see. So what did you do?"

Horvath's lips shaped a cynical smile. "Luckily Sandor is an expert safecracker. So I had him remove the brooch from Shand's possession."

"And then I came along and upset the applecart." Nancy said coolly. "And just how do you expect to get rid of my boyfriend and me without getting caught?"

Horvath explained that his chauffeur would slip away from Ned Nickerson in the darkness, then put on his "Sweeney Flint" disguise and let himself be glimpsed by Ned. Nothing more would be seen of Sandor, however, thus causing Ned to assume the chauffeur had fallen victim to the crook. "And when your boyfriend returns to the house, he'll find me lying on the floor, apparently stunned from a blow on the head."

"No doubt you'll tell him I was seized and carried off by Sweeney Flint," guessed Nancy.

"Exactly, my dear! There happens to be a cave

on this island with an underground lake that connects with the sea outside. Evidence will be found indicating that you and Sandor were taken there, and your bodies dumped into that lake."

"How clever! Sandor will come back to life someday—suitably disguised, of course—when you finally come to hire a new chauffeur."

"Correct!" Horvath beamed maliciously. But a sudden noise at the window distracted him. "What's going on out there?" he muttered.

"I suspect Sandor just discovered Ned eavesdropping at the window," Nancy said calmly, "so now Ned's fighting him off."

"*What!*" Horvath glared at the girl.

"Surely you didn't expect me to come out to Moonlight Island and walk into your spiderweb without taking precautions, once I began to suspect you were the real criminal?" said Nancy. "I warned Ned we'd better stay in close touch and not get separated, so he probably came straight back to the house as soon as he and Sandor separated to begin searching."

With an angry exclamation, Horvath pressed a switch. The grounds were at once bathed in floodlights. As Horvath flung back the curtains, Ned could be seen struggling fiercely with Sandor!

Horvath opened the window and grabbed a brass candlestick to attack the husky young man. It was an unwise move. Nancy snatched at the small Oriental carpet under Horvath's feet and pulled it, causing him to fall. He hit his head, and with a faint mutter, sank into unconsciousness.

Just then Ned landed a hard punch to the jaw that sent Sandor crashing among the shrubbery!

"Oh, Ne-e-ed!" gasped Nancy in a trembling voice as he gathered her in his arms.

Within an hour, the state police had arrived on the island, and the two were safely on their way back to the mainland. Although Nancy found herself wondering about her next adventure, one that would lead to *The Haunted Carousel*, she was happy for the moment just to feel Ned's kiss on her cheek and hear his whispering voice call her "my sweet little mystery-solver!"

You are invited to join

THE OFFICIAL NANCY DREW ®/
HARDY BOYS ® FAN CLUB!

Be the first in your neighborhood to find out
about the newest adventures of Nancy, Frank,
and Joe in the **Nancy Drew** ®/ **Hardy Boys** ®
**Mystery Reporter,** and to receive your official
membership card. Just send your name, age,
address, and zip code on a postcard *only* to:

**The Official Nancy Drew ®/**
**Hardy Boys ® Fan Club**
**Wanderer Books**
**Simon & Schuster Building**
**1230 Avenue of the Americas**
**New York, New York 10020**

OFFER VALID ONLY IN THE UNITED STATES.

# NANCY DREW MYSTERY STORIES®
## by Carolyn Keene

**You will also enjoy**

# THE LINDA CRAIG® SERIES
## by Ann Sheldon